TOUCHED
BY
SHADOWS

VAUGHN A. JACKSON

JOURNALSTONE
YOUR LINK TO ARTIST TALENT

ISBN: 978-1-68510-011-7 (sc)
ISBN: 978-1-68510-012-4 (ebook)
Library of Congress Control Number: 2021946937

First printing edition: December 10, 2021
Published by JournalStone Publishing in the United States of America.
Cover Design: Don Noble
Proofreading and Cover/Interior Layout by Scarlett R. Algee
Editing by Sean Leonard

JournalStone Publishing
3205 Sassafras Trail
Carbondale, Illinois 62901

JournalStone books may be ordered through booksellers or by contacting:
JournalStone | www.journalstone.com

To my parents, who always believed in me.
To my girlfriend, who told me this story was good enough to submit.
And to my two kittens who kept my feet warm, and full of teeth and claws, as I wrote.
Thank you.

TOUCHED
BY
SHADOWS

CHAPTER 1

THE BANGING FROM inside the diving bell no longer echoed throughout the lab as it was lowered inch by inch into the viscous fluid of the immersion tank.

"October 10, 1974." Dr. Bachman spoke into his tape recorder as Lawrence watched him pace around the laboratory. He stopped behind a wide console that faced the tank. "Human experiment attempt number" — he paused before continuing with greater confidence — "the final experiment. Today we will succeed."

Lawrence fingered the burn on his face from one of their previous, unprepared attempts. He knew the girl didn't mean to do it, but the electrical fire she'd started had been dangerous all the same. If he closed his eyes, he could still feel the pain searing down into his skull and smell the overpowering scent of burning flesh. His stomach turned at the thought. *Today will be different*, he thought. *We've triple checked everything.*

"We cannot afford any miscalculations or other mistakes. This time we must be *perfect*." The lead scientist's crooked frame peered down over the main console as he rasped. "Is everything prepared?"

Lawrence hurried around the room, dodging the equally frantic movements of his fellow lab assistants, checking gauges, pulse readings, and every manner of sensor. Red lights flashed on one panel. He flipped a switch and the lights turned a solid green. He tapped on a gauge whose needle wavered back and forth. It grew steady and maintained its position on the indicator. All of the equipment circled around the tank in the center, making it easy to watch the machinery and the subject. As he went, he checked off items on the list on his clipboard.

"All green here," he said, scanning the room to see that the others also gave a positive status check. He cast another glance at the submerged container. "Do we go, Doctor Bachman?"

A wet breath ragged with excitement escaped the old man's lungs. "Now," he said. "Lead us to the source of your power, Oumou." He flipped the master switch. The lights dimmed and then returned to their original brightness.

Despite the tangible excitement in the room, no one clapped or cheered as the switches were flipped. A collective held breath silenced the room. Each of them knew that this was a moment for absolute focus. Lawrence noticed his knuckles whitening from the grip on his clipboard. He made a concerted effort to relax.

The fluid in the tank rippled softly for a few seconds before once again becoming placid. Lawrence's chest strained against the urge to exhale. They couldn't allow even the slightest disturbance. When the water became absolutely still, Lawrence gave a thumbs-up to Dr. Bachman. The older scientist nodded in acknowledgment. He turned a dial on his console. A mosquito noise filled the room. Dr. Bachman pressed a button on his console.

The still water sparked to life with electricity. It bubbled and hissed as arcs of lightning danced across the dark blue surface. Dr. Bachman folded his hands behind his back. "And now we wait."

The entire room did just that. No sound but the hum of electricity filled Lawrence's senses, numbing them and feeling as though an itch was breaking out over his entire body. He knew that if his anxiety responded like this, the girl in the tank had no chance to maintain her calm. High anxiety triggered the most powerful of her outbursts, and that was what they needed. Dr. Bachman called it "opening the door." As he thought about that conversation, a chill ran down Lawrence's spine and a single thought crossed his mind: *What's on the other side?*

The tank and diving bell were reinforced to the height of what money and science could provide. Lawrence glanced up at Dr. Bachman. The man's eyes burned with manic passion as he observed his experiment in action. Lawrence had to wonder if he ever once thought about the girl inside as a person. But then again, had he?

"Activate the pulse," came the old man's voice once more.

Lawrence did as he was told, turning the dial on the machine to his right until he could feel the subsonic pulse like a second heartbeat. He hated the pulse, ringing in the depths of his core like a nervous breakdown waiting to happen. Like something clawing its way up from the depths of your subconscious and demanding to be let out. Stepping away from the machine did nothing to ease the discomfort. *How long do we have to wait? Just give us some—*

The sound of metal bending and warping screamed out into the room. And then, without warning, the entire immersion tank collapsed in on itself like a crumpled ball of aluminum. The whole room froze in a stunned silence. Lawrence barely had time to react as the machine that controlled the pulse burst into flames before detonating with the force of a bomb. Shrapnel, sparks, and smoke sprayed out into the room. One of the other assistants turned just in time for a sheet of metal the size of a dinner plate to embed itself in her head. She dropped to the floor, and red pooled around her body.

The other machines followed suit, combusting before exploding and spraying the panicked scientists with deadly debris. Another explosion finally shorted the lab's circuits and the room was plunged into darkness. There was a sound in the darkness; not a scream, like

Lawrence expected from the girl, but an echoing moan. The sound grew until it drowned out any other thoughts he might have. He clamped his hands over his ears but could still hear it as it wailed at the center of the room. He instinctively took a step towards the door.

A figure shrouded in smoke and darkness rose up from the back of the laboratory. *The girl? No,* Lawrence thought as it moved towards him. Disproportionate limbs dangled from a hunched-over form. It turned a horned head towards them. Lawrence wanted to scream.

The figure moved wrong, as if one second it was there and then the next it was elsewhere. It was impossible to focus on, seeming to shift and swirl with the smoke. It appeared next to a cowering scientist and raised what appeared to be its head like a cobra preparing to strike, before plunging itself entirely down the young man's throat. His eyes rolled back into his skull and he seized violently before collapsing to the ground, blood trickling from the corners of his mouth. The man's death flipped a switch in the room. Doctor Bachman, Lawrence, and the two remaining scientists made a panicked sprint to the door. Lawrence only heard the sounds of what happened to the two behind him. He dared not turn around. Ahead of him, Doctor Bachman tripped, his brittle body slamming to the ground with a pained gasp. Lawrence considered stopping to help the man but heard the *thing* rustling right behind him. It was so close he could smell it, like a rotting corpse. He closed his eyes as he ran past the crumpled form on the ground, getting to the door and slamming it behind him. Lawrence could only watch from behind the glass window as the shadow creature wound its way around the old man's form and crushed him like a constrictor about to eat its prey.

Realization struck Lawrence as he looked around. He was the last man standing. From behind the glass, the creature raised itself up to regard him with an evil, jagged smile, uneven teeth piercing from a wide mouth. Lawrence doubled over, head in his hands, as an electric hum scraped at the back of his skull. The creature pressed itself against the glass and stared at him. Lawrence closed his eyes and waited for the end. But nothing happened. He opened his eyes again and saw that the creature was gone. It was just him, and a lab full of fire, smoke, and burning corpses. A slick film of sweat coated his entire body and soaked through his shirt. His knees gave out and he slumped to the ground.

* * *

Lawrence hadn't slept in three days. He turned the small pistol over in his hands and ran his thumb over the polished wood handle and up to the hammer, miming the action of cocking the gun. It wasn't his, not originally. Nothing in this office was. He'd found the gun in a drawer on the desk. His new desk. The late Dr. Bachman's desk.

The death of all of your colleagues lends itself well to a promotion, he thought bitterly.

The desk felt too big for the tiny office. Six feet of solid mahogany wedged in the middle of the room made it feel more desk than office. If he wanted out, he had to shuffle around through that tiny space between the wall and the desk. If he didn't already think he had no right to be here, the presence of such an elitist barrier between him and anyone who entered the office really drove the point home. This wasn't his office; it belonged to a dead man.

What was that thing? he thought.

His eyes darted around the room, lingering on every shadow cast by the light at his desk, praying that it didn't move. He'd shuttered the blinds to keep the sun from stretching out the shadows as it moved across the sky. Even with just the light from the desk lamp, the shadows were all too deep. He picked up the lamp and scanned the room, illuminating every corner, but in the process casting deeper, darker shadows all around. A shiver ran down his spine, and he slammed the lamp on the desk with a shout. Beads of sweat rolled down his forehead, stinging his eyes. He sunk deep into the luxurious leather chair, trying with all his might to disappear into its plush cushion.

Someone rapped violently on the frosted glass pane of the office door. Lawrence stifled a shriek. A shadowy figure waited a minute before pounding its fist on the glass once more. Lawrence aimed the gun at the glass.

"Doctor Calburn, we're with the FBI," the figure called.

"Prove it," Lawrence said, his hands shaking so violently he could barely maintain his aim.

"We spoke on the phone," the figure said. "Told you we'd be out today."

Lawrence swallowed hard. He placed the gun on a nearby stack of papers and wiped the sweat from his brow. He shuffled around the desk and unlocked the door.

"Come in." He squeezed himself back behind the desk and into his chair.

Two suits hidden behind dark sunglasses and wide-brimmed hats strolled into the room. A frustrated air of arrogance clouded around them thicker than the smoke that billowed from their cigarettes.

"Thank you for seeing us," the first agent said. He flashed his badge so quickly Lawrence didn't get a chance to see it before he shoved it back in the pocket of his suit jacket.

"Took you long enough," the second agent said as he filed into the room behind his partner. He lounged against the door with his hands buried deep in his pockets. The man puffed on his cigarette and looked as if he wanted to be anywhere but here. Lawrence felt the same. With the three of them in the room, there was hardly space to breathe let alone stand to offer a handshake.

"Your names?" Lawrence asked.

"Don't matter," said the man leaning against the door.

"I see." Lawrence remained seated and willed himself not to fumble his words. "How can I help you?"

"Got a lot of bodies down at the morgue, Doctor Calburn. Lots of bodies." The man chewed the butt of his cigarette as he spoke.

"Actually, I'm not a doctor, I'm an—"

The partner spoke up. "Did it sound like he asked?"

"No." Lawrence glanced at the pistol on the desk. He cursed himself for not putting it back where he found it. "You're here about the accident?"

"Well," the first agent said, "we're not here to throw you a party. Why don't you tell us what happened? From the beginning."

"I wrote it all in my report—"

"We read your report," the partner said. "But writing makes lying easy. Talking," he pushed past his partner and leaned over the desk to press a finger into Lawrence's chest, "that's not as easy, is it?" He punctuated the last two words with harsh jabs of his pointed finger. Lawrence winced at the pain.

"No, I suppose not," he said, rubbing his chest. "Well, like I said, the experiment—"

"What kind of experiments do you do here, doctor?" The first agent blew a stream of smoke into Lawrence's face that made him sputter and cough.

Lawrence froze. *They don't know.* His mouth went dry. *They'll put me away forever.* He forced himself to regain composure. "We study the human brain," he said.

"Hmm, psychology," the partner said.

"Neurology, actually," Lawrence said. He received a glare from behind a pair of lowered shades and a grunt for his trouble.

"So how did you go from grey matter to blood splatter?" the first agent asked, snapping his fingers to get Lawrence's attention.

Lie, Lawrence's mind screamed at him. *Lie!*

"Equipment malfunction," Lawrence said at last.

"Excuse me?" the first agent said, with a skeptical glance to his partner.

"Our sensors require a lot of power, electricity," Lawrence continued. "There was a short in the wiring that caused a fire to break out and detonate some of our larger machinery." He swallowed hard. "You'll find a lot of the corpses have shrapnel damage beneath the burns." Images of his colleagues' deaths rushed through his mind. He fought down a wave of nausea and prayed he didn't look as miserable as he felt.

The two agents eyed him, shared a look with each other, and nodded in silent agreement before the lead agent spoke again. "I see," he said. "Well, you best know that there will be a full investigation into the deaths of your colleagues *as well* as into your status as the sole survivor."

"He means don't leave town," the partner added.

Lawrence forced a smile. "Of course. Is that all?"

"Yes, I think so, for now at least," the lead agent said with a smile devoid of any semblance of warmth. "We'll be in touch."

Lawrence shuffled his way around the desk, past the agents, and opened the office door. "Then have a nice day," he said. "As you can imagine, there is a lot to be done around here."

"Doctor," the agent said, tipping his hat as he exited.

His partner tipped his hat without a word and followed suit. Lawrence watched them stroll down the hallway and turn the corner leading to the facility exit. He closed the door and slumped against it. He exhaled and leaned back in his chair with his hands cupping his face.

"I thought they'd never leave," he said.

In the returned quiet, his thoughts wandered back to the pistol on the desk. *If they blame me...* He took a deep breath and sat back at the desk, reaching hesitantly for the gun. *I'm done. They'll never believe what happened.* His fingers glided over the polished silver.

Just as he was about to take it in his hand, he heard a rustling noise from the back corner of the room. The smell of rot and mildew filled the air. Lawrence's stomach dropped. He jerked his head around and saw nothing but a shadow that blanketed the corner in darkness. His heart pounded in his chest as he realized that the light from the lamp should have illuminated that space completely. The darkness was too deep to be a regular shadow anyway, and as he stared at it, it shifted and squirmed, rising to its full height, a whole head above Lawrence.

He wanted to scream, but he remembered the creature forcing itself down the throat of one of the others. Instead, he clamped his hand over his mouth and grabbed the gun, sending a flutter of papers into the air. His arm trembled wildly as he fired off his first shot. It missed, splintering the wooden wall. The creature took a janky step towards him, reaching out a clawed hand. Lawrence fired again. The bullet struck the creature dead center, tearing a hole so wide that Lawrence could see right through it. He gasped. The creature paused and looked down at the gaping hole in its chest. Within seconds the wound had sealed shut and the creature focused its attention back on Lawrence.

"Stay away," Lawrence said. He shot the creature three more times, each bullet tearing a hole in the creature's shadowy form. Within seconds each hole vanished like it had never existed. With a panicked gasp, Lawrence pressed the barrel of the gun against his own head.

Before he could pull the trigger, the thing was on him, suffocating him in its darkness. The gun clattered to the ground, firing its last shot uselessly into the floorboards. Lawrence felt the creature seeping into him. It felt as if all the life in him was being wrung out and replaced with the entity's presence. The world around him shifted and changed, at once the office of the late Doctor Bachman, but also another place, a place of nothingness. His mind was slipping. There was a voice drowning out his thoughts, demanding control. *I... don't...want...*

Lawrence was gone, and in his place stood the dark thing in his body, grinning like a demon at its own reflection. It traced a hand along the burn on its new face and thought, *This will do, for now.*

CHAPTER 2

THE DARKNESS OF the tank hadn't scared Oumou for a while. She got used to it so quick she had even surprised herself. This time had been different though. The whispering voice, the one that beckoned to her from the darkness inside the tank, got under her skin. It made her want to run. To scream. She'd scrunched her eyes closed and talked to herself until she felt like she was screaming, just to drown out the disembodied sound. The voice had gone quiet, and so had the world outside. Nothing but the sound of her own screaming. The sudden silence had sent panic like electricity through her veins. No, the darkness isn't what scared her, it was the feeling of something watching her. Hunting her. The darkness had been her place to hide, but now it was no longer safe, and so Oumou had wished herself away.

The diving bell cracked into existence with an echoing pop. Yellow-tinted light flooded into the dark confined space through the one circular viewport. Oumou pressed her face against the glass and saw that she was in a field of vines. As she leaned forward against the door, it creaked and fell open with a dull thud. A soft breeze caressed her face. It carried with it the smell of wet dirt and verdant plant life. She couldn't remember the last time she'd smelled anything but the antiseptic smell of the lab. She took a hesitant step outside, her toes sinking into the warm and loamy soil. She squinted and looked up at the bright golden sun illuminating a baby blue sky. The brightness burned her eyes, and she flinched away. *Where am I?*

She stood at the center of a row of vines high enough that she couldn't see over them. Thin vapors of steam rose lazily from the diving bell. She watched them dissipate into the air. Taking one wobbly step at a time, she paced the row up and down. She tripped over a stray vine. When she stood up again, her paper-thin medical robe was smeared with the loose soil, turning it a dingy brown. The mud clung to her robe in heavy clumps that she tried her best to brush off. Oumou struggled to take in her surroundings, but it was all so overwhelming. Rows and rows of fence posts covered in lush green vines strung from thin wire surrounded her, stretching out as far as she could see in every direction. Small green fruit hung low and heavy with juice. She reached out a hand and plucked one free.

"Grapes," she said in a hushed voice.

"Hello?" a girl's voice called.

Oumou looked frantically for a place to hide. Seeing no better option, she scurried back into the diving bell and hoped the other person wouldn't see it. With her back to the door, she crouched into a ball and covered her head with her hands.

"Is someone there?" The girl sounded young. "I thought I heard you fall. Are you okay? Do you need help?"

Oumou heard the rustling of the nearby vines. She glanced over her shoulder in time to see a crown of blonde hair peek into the opening of the container, followed by two piercing blue eyes.

"Hello?" the girl called. "Are you in here?"

"Go away," Oumou said.

"That's rude," the girl said, pouting. "Can I come in?"

"No."

The girl pouted harder. "Please?" she said, drawing out the middle of the word as long as she could before taking a breath to start again.

Resigned, Oumou answered. "Yes."

A tiny, excited gasp, a quick shuffling of feet, and the girl crawled into the diving bell alongside Oumou.

"There's not a lot of room in here," she said.

"No," Oumou said.

"Let's go outside again," she said. "Come on." She grabbed Oumou by the hand and pulled her back out into the vineyard. Oumou resisted, and the girl's hand slipped, sending her tumbling into the dirt. Oumou shuffled nervously as she watched the girl bounce back up and look down at her now dirty outfit.

"Mom won't be happy," she said with a grimace. "She just said not to get this dirty. Oops." She looked back up to Oumou and her face brightened. "Anyway, my name's Amanda," she chirped, her hand shooting out in front of her.

Oumou stared and frowned a little. The area around Amanda's mouth was sticky with the remains of the grapes that filled the field around them. Her hands were the same.

Amanda pouted once more. "It's rude not to shake hands and introduce yourself, you know?"

"Oh," Oumou stuttered, "uh, sorry?" She held out her hand, reluctant to grasp the other girl's sticky fingers in her own. Just as she was about to clasp the outstretched hand, a sharp pain sparked in her head. Her face and limbs went numb. She wobbled on the spot as stars flashed all the colors of the rainbow before her eyes.

"Are you okay?" Amanda asked. "You look a little...not...okay?"

"I..." Oumou started, but snapped her mouth shut when she felt like she might throw up. Her vision began to blur on the edges and a velvety darkness threatened to consume her. "No," she whimpered, but it made no difference. Her knees gave out first, tipping her forward. She blinked and felt herself falling, falling, falling...

She slammed into the dirt face-first.

"Are you okay?" Amanda asked.

Oumou didn't respond. Her body lay there silent.

"Hey," Amanda said, "get up. You're scaring me."

Oumou was silent.

"This isn't funny. I don't like it."

Still nothing.

Her fear began to choke her up. "Get up, please."

A small pool of blood began forming around where Oumou's nose struck the ground. The site of the red liquid pushed Amanda over the edge.

"Mom, Dad!" she screamed. "Help!"

The vines rustled and her parents rushed up behind their daughter.

"What's the matter, sweetie?" Her father knelt down beside her.

Amanda's breathing came quick and shallow and she couldn't find it in herself to make any more words. She pointed at the girl on the ground in front of her and let out the tiniest whimper.

"My God." Her mother gasped and beckoned Amanda into her arms, where she pulled her into a tight hug, shielding her eyes against her chest. "Is she dead, Harold?" she whispered.

Harold slid down into the crater and placed two fingers against Oumou's neck. "Her pulse is weak, but she's alive. She must have fainted."

"But look at the dirt," Elizabeth argued. "Is that blood?"

Harold rolled Oumou over, taking care to stabilize her head and neck. He pointed to her nose. "Her nose," he said. "Might be broken, might not be. Those injuries always bleed quite profusely."

Elizabeth let out a sigh of relief. "What should we do with her?"

Harold looked at Oumou's stained hospital gown. He stood up, peering over the vines and searching the surrounding area. "I don't see anyone else out here," he said. "And the nearest hospital is miles away."

"You don't think she walked all the way here, do you?" his wife asked.

He dragged his hand along the metal diving bell. "Any idea what this is?"

Elizabeth shook her head.

"Yeah, me neither." He looked down at Oumou, laid out on her back. Her breaths were deep and even. "Let's get her back to the house so I can give her a proper once over."

"Are you sure it's safe?"

"She's just a kid," Harold said. "And besides, as a doctor..."

"You couldn't just leave her here, I know," Elizabeth said. "You're right anyway, she's a kid, and she needs help."

Harold hoisted Oumou into his arms. "She probably just needs some rest. Once she wakes up, we'll see if we can get her back to her parents. It'll be okay."

Amanda pulled away from her mother. She was calmer now, and hearing that the other girl was not dead had restored a portion of her bravery. "I'm gonna walk beside Dad," she said defiantly. "To make sure he doesn't drop her!"

* * *

Oumou Beverly woke up in a bed, in a room, in a house, none of which she recognized. This alone unsettled her enough, and the throbbing pain that radiated throughout her face didn't help. Full blown panic didn't truly set in until the door began to crack open. She shifted under the scratchy sheets, hiding, as soft footsteps followed by heavier footsteps entered into the room. Oumou shifted her head out of the blankets when the noises stopped. She stared at the blonde girl with sky blue eyes, who in turn was staring back at her. Her thin cherry lips spread into a wide, gap-toothed smile.

"Mom, Dad, she woke up! She's awake!" the girl shouted, jumping up and down before rushing to Oumou's bedside. "Hi, my name's Amanda. What's your name? Where are you from? Does your nose hurt? Do you like cats? I've always wanted a cat. What were you doing in the pit? Why did you faint?"

Oumou barely had time to register all the questions being hurled at her before another, sterner voice cut in. "Amanda, honey, give the girl some space. She's probably still exhausted from her accident." A tall man with dark blonde hair entered the room, his white labcoat hanging down to his legs. He looked at Oumou. "How do you feel?"

Oumou screamed. The door slammed shut and the bed rocked violently from side to side.

Amanda jumped, and her dad looked on in panicked confusion. There was a rush of footsteps, followed by a third, calming voice.

"What's wrong?" the woman asked, bursting into the room. She elbowed her way past the man in the labcoat and took Oumou's hands in her own. Their warmth dragged Oumou back into the room and out of her fear, if only a little. Her breaths still came in quick succession, and her wide eyes darted around the room.

"I don't know, she took one look at me and started wailing." The man in the labcoat shrugged, eyes wide and brow raised.

"Well, get out then." She shooed the man, who still looked just as confused, out of the room and closed the door after him. The woman approached the bedside and took Oumou's hands back in hers. "There, there," she said. "What's wrong, sweetie?"

Oumou coughed, her voice giving out from the scream. She wiped at the tears running down her face, and accidentally bumped her nose, which only served to cause more tears to well up in her eyes. "White coats." The two words were punctuated by a whistling sniff and, due to her broken nose, sounded more like nasally gibberish than actual words. "Bad."

"No, no, sweetie, he just wants to help you. He's the one who patched up your nose."

Oumou gingerly put a finger on her nose and felt the stiff cotton of the bandages. It throbbed a lot, but it didn't hurt that bad. Unless she touched it too hard, or sniffed, she realized as the most recent one sent warm pain radiating through her skull. "He helped me?"

"Yeah, he did. Amanda, go tell your father to take off his coat and come back in."

The blonde girl, who'd been standing in the corner, staring wide-eyed, nodded her head quickly and bounced out the door. A few seconds later, the man returned in just a grey turtleneck and blue jeans.

He adjusted his glasses awkwardly. "Hey, kiddo, sorry if I frightened you earlier."

Oumou nodded slowly, eyeing the man suspiciously. "Thank you for..." She rubbed her bandaged nose between two fingers, just barely touching it.

"No need to thank me, I'm a doctor, it's what I do."

"I don't think I like doctors," Oumou mumbled.

The man chuckled. "Not many people do."

"But you seem...okay," she added.

The man gave a half-smile. "That is the greatest compliment I have received all day," he said wryly. The woman shot him a look and he added, "Sorry, sorry."

"What were you doing in a pit out with the grapes?" Amanda stepped from behind her father.

A look of confusion crossed Oumou's face. "What?"

"Amanda found you out in the vineyard just outside of town," the woman said.

"Oh." Oumou looked down at the blanket covering her lower body. "I was running away."

The woman covered her mouth with a hand. "From what?"

"White coats." Oumou didn't look up, but her grip on the blankets tightened.

The man and woman shared a concerned look. "Mental hospital?" she mouthed to him.

Oumou didn't know what the woman meant, so she stayed quiet during the exchange.

"Maybe," came the man's silent reply. His face grew serious. He knelt down beside the woman at the bedside and said, "You're safe here, okay?"

Oumou forced a smile and nodded, even though she didn't believe what the man was saying. She thought about the darkness of the tank, of the silence that suffocated her, and the voice that had called to her from the void. Whatever it was hadn't felt safe.

CHAPTER 3

"YOU PLANNING ON leaving anytime soon, boy?" The bartender peered over the glass he'd been toweling for the past ten minutes.

"Bar don't close 'til two," Leslie Johnson said, taking another sip of his whiskey. He glanced at the clock on the wall. One forty-five. "Besides, you going to ask them when they plan on leaving?" He jerked his thumb in the direction of an all-white group of partygoers finishing their tenth round. Eleventh if you counted the shots.

"Them, I like. You—"

"Not so much, huh?"

The bartender gave no visible response.

"And what's not to like about me?" Leslie leaned back and gripped the lapels on his blazer. A smug grin spread across his face. "Ain't I just dandy, mister?"

The bartender scowled.

"Mhmm, see? Ain't a damn thing wrong with me except the color of my skin, and you're pissed you can't even say that out loud anymore, aren't you?" He chuckled dryly and finished the last bit of whiskey in his glass.

The bartender ground his teeth so hard Leslie thought they might crack. He could practically hear the strain in the man's jaw as he spoke. "You want to leave. Right. Now."

"Now that, that right there, is God's truth. But first..." He lifted the camera hanging from his neck. A flash lit the dim of the bar, much to the chagrin of the drunk partygoers. They grumpily muttered something as he reached the door. One of them cheered, before being hushed by his friends. "Money's under the glass," Leslie said, "a small apology for the review you'll have in the paper tomorrow. You'll like it less than you liked me." He swept his hand dramatically through the air. "Chuck's Bar: Where an ill-tempered racist serves you piss instead of whiskey. Zero stars."

Leslie ducked just in time to avoid a glass bottle that instead exploded against the wall behind where his head had been. That was his cue to leave. He quickly ducked out the door, hung a right and sprinted into the nearest alley he could find. His knife slid silently into the palm of his hand and snapped open with a flick of his wrist. He hoped to God it wouldn't come to violence. The bartender's obscene cries echoed around him, but no lumbering footsteps followed him into the alley. He heard the bar door slam, and the night returned to the normal hum of New York activity.

Leslie sighed. The slight buzz of the whiskey evaporated into the cool night air with each rapid thump of his heartbeat. "Sometimes you push things too far, man." He tucked his arms around himself and set off for home. Nighttime in the city was still no safe place for a black man. *Just 'cause the government says you're a person, doesn't mean anyone's gotta agree.* The bitter thought hung in his mind while he ducked past cops and lone travelers on his way back to the cramped, one-room apartment he called home.

Inside, he locked the door, kicked off his shoes, and flopped down onto his bed.

* * *

The moistened cling of his sheets didn't register at first, only the panic of darkness and the foul taste of a lingering nightmare. Leslie's eyes sprang open. It felt like something was perched on his chest trying to suffocate him. His mind thrashed and raged, but his body refused to move. He tried to scream, but no sound came out. There was something at the foot of his bed. He couldn't see it, but he could feel it watching him. All he could do was stare at the ceiling and wait for it to end. The sound of his heartbeat was deafening. Every time he thought he was about to suffocate, his body took an involuntary gasp of air, and the whole process started over. Slowly, his body began to respond to his commands. He wiggled a finger first, and then a toe. The pressure on his chest began to relent. He gulped down air in greedy breaths. As the fear-induced paralysis ebbed away, it began to take the details of the nightmare with it. When he could finally move, he scribbled three words on the notepad by his bedside before the last memory of the dream faded. For not the first time in his life, Leslie Johnson disentangled himself from soaking wet sheets and made his way, still shaking, to his phone.

"Jesus, Les, do you know what time it is?" The voice on the other end of the phone yawned.

"No." His voice sounded hollow, wrong even to his own ears.

"It's" — the voice hesitated — "it happened again?"

"Archwood, North Carolina," Leslie mumbled. "You heard of it?"

"Man, you got to stop doing this to yourself. See a shrink, or an exorcist, or something. Last time you didn't eat for a week. It's not healthy."

"Ray," Leslie snapped. *It's not like I have a fucking choice.* "Have you heard of it?"

A sigh of resignation crackled through the phone. Leslie heard the rustle of papers on the line, and finally. "Small town. Real small. Situated right next to a state-owned vineyard. Honestly, aside from that, it's nothing. A blip. Doesn't even show up on half the maps I have."

"Thank you." Leslie jotted the scraps of information on the notepad beneath the town's name. "I'm going."

"Maybe you should sit this one out, man. I mean, our folk down in the middle of nowhere South? That sound right to you?"

Leslie ignored him. "Tell Dick I won't be coming in. I'll explain when I get back. May even have a story when I get back."

Silence on the line.

"Ray?"

"Yeah, yeah, I'll tell him. Should I plan your funeral while I'm at it? Just in case?"

"Why bother? Nobody would come." He hung up before the man on the other end could respond.

Afraid to close his eyes and discover what lurked in his dreams a second time, Leslie sat in darkness until the sun came up. He checked to make sure his camera had enough film, packed a spare outfit, skipped breakfast, and headed straight for the airport.

CHAPTER 4

OUMOU STILL DIDN'T trust Mr. Chastaine, even though he no longer wore his white coat around her. The few times she'd caught him in it, he made sure to take it off immediately and assure her that he meant no harm. And every time, Oumou nodded and watched him with the same distrustful gaze.

Mrs. Chastaine made her feel comfortable enough, but Oumou was skeptical of her as well. Nobody had ever been as nice to her. She wondered if she was trying to get her to lower her guard. *And then more experiments,* Oumou thought.

After getting over the initial shock of Oumou's breakdown, Amanda had not left her side. Every second with her it was another question, another topic of conversation, or another fit of unprompted giggling.

"You're my first friend, you know?" she said, as they sat on the floor of the downstairs guest room. The comment came out of nowhere and at first Oumou didn't even register what was said. "Here," she said, gently pulling Oumou towards an antique dollhouse on the back wall of her room. She opened the house and dolls and figures of all kinds spilled onto the floor. "We can play with these!"

"But we just met," Oumou replied, examining the female dolls. None of them looked like her.

"I know, but that's okay, we can be fast friends, like Mom always says."

Oumou's eyes lingered on a black doll dressed in a splotchy green and brown pattern.

Amanda followed her gaze and said, "That one's the bad guy."

"Why?"

"He's a thug. That's what Miss Sylvia always says. Thugs are bad guys."

"Who's that?"

"She helps out the church a lot. Mom lets me play with these sometimes, so I stay quiet. Miss Sylvia saw and that's when she told me." The girl smiled innocently.

"Oh." Oumou moved to put the doll down, but changed her mind, holding him up in front of her face. "What if he wants to be a good guy?"

Amanda paused in the middle of brushing her doll's hair, cocked her head to the side, and said, "Okay. I guess no one's always a bad guy."

Oumou smiled down at the figure in her hand. She followed what Amanda was doing and dragged a small plastic brush back and forth over the man's short plastic hair.

"He's going to be really pretty," Amanda said with a giggle.

"Yeah," Oumou said, "I guess." She gave an awkward smile.

Mrs. Chastaine peeked her head around the door. "Hey, girls, come on, we're going to go shopping. I'm sure Oumou doesn't want to be stuck in that dirty thing all day." She gestured to the muck-stained hospital robe hanging loosely on Oumou's thin frame.

Amanda bolted up and let out a long, drawn-out, "Yay. Can I get something too?"

"We'll see," Mrs. Chastaine said, "but this trip is for Oumou, okay?"

Amanda nodded her head excitedly. "Mhmm."

Oumou rose and shuffled her feet, her hands folded in front of her. She stared at the ground and wrung her hands, her toy discarded on the floor next to Amanda's.

"What's wrong, Oumou?" Mrs. Chastaine looked at the girl for a second before slapping her palm against her forehead. "Of course, you can't go out like that."

"That's not—"

"Don't worry, I'll grab you something of Amanda's to wear for now," she said.

"But—"

Mrs. Chastaine had already disappeared into Amanda's closet, focused on sifting through the several hanging outfits Oumou could make out past the woman's frame.

Amanda looked at Oumou, cocking her head so that her golden curls shimmered. "You don't like shopping?"

"Never been."

"You've never been shopping?" Amanda's eyes widened and she pulled Oumou into a tight hug.

"What are you doing?" Oumou asked, squirming against the blonde girl's arms.

"Hugging."

"Why?"

"I don't know. I was sad because you've never been shopping, and I didn't want you to be sad, so I hugged you."

Oumou clamored her way out of the other girl's grip and stood just off to the side, out of arm's reach.

By now, Mrs. Chastaine had spun around with a little pink dress that she helped Oumou into while Amanda watched. She scrubbed a bit of dirt from Oumou's face and made an attempt at taming the girl's hair, gave up, and put the entire puff into one hair-tie, leaving Oumou with a single frizzy ponytail.

"You're so pretty," the other girl said, clapping her hands and bouncing up and down.

"I don't want to go shopping." Oumou said, tugging uncomfortably at the bottom of the frilly thing she found herself in.

"Oh, Oumou, the bad men won't find you here," Mrs. Chastaine said, placing a hand on Oumou's shoulder. "Now come on, let's go." She guided Oumou by the shoulder and together the three of them walked out of the front door.

* * *

Oumou counted around twenty buildings as they walked the pebbly road towards a building near the center of the town. A sign in the center of the town announced "Archwood, North Carolina" in crisp white letters. Beneath that the current population of fifty-eight people was stamped in the same white lettering, only smaller. The last line on the sign read, "May God Keep Our Town Pure."

"What does that mean?" she asked.

"Hm?" Mrs. Chastaine said before glancing at the sign. "Oh, it just means we don't want any bad people here," she said.

To Oumou's discomfort, they were stopped numerous times between the Chastaine household and their destination. The first passersby were a tight-lipped woman named Leah Buckett and her husband, a gruff man knotted with muscle. What he lacked in height, he made up for in width. He barely grunted an acknowledgement when Mrs. Chastaine introduced the young girl. Leah, on the other hand, was polite, but quickly made an excuse and hurried her husband along their path.

Halfway to the building with clothes in the front window, a young woman stepped out of a building, saw the three of them and waved.

"Vicki," Mrs. Chastaine said, pulling the woman into a warm embrace. "Down here looking to see what books the deliveries brought in?"

Vicki adjusted her glasses, knocked askew by the sudden show of affection, and said, "I heard they would have some older books this time, so I had to check for myself." She held up a stack of four books that Oumou thought might fall apart right in front of all of them. "The one on top is a Bible, but the one on the bottom," she fanned herself, "well, not everyone in history was a stick in the mud."

Mrs. Chastaine smiled politely.

Vicki ceased her fanning and noticed Oumou for the first time. "Oh! Hello. Who might you be?"

Oumou shot a nervous glance at Mrs. Chastaine, then, realizing what she'd done, stared a burning hole into the ground at her feet.

"This is Oumou," Mrs. Chastaine said. "We—"

"You don't owe me an explanation," Vicki said, "but it's nice to meet you, Oumou. You probably heard, but my name is Vicki. Do you want a jellybean?" The young woman reached into her coat pocket and pulled out a handful of colorful candies.

Oumou reached out a nervous hand and plucked a bright red one from the center of Vicki's hand. She twirled it in her fingers, taking in the shape and the blue flecks of color that dotted its surface. Amanda also reached out and grabbed a candy. Oumou watched as she popped it into her mouth. She did the same. The sweet taste of strawberry filled her mouth and stung the insides of her cheeks. She shivered with joy.

"Oh shit."

Oumou looked up to see a round man whose forehead glistened with sweat. The stains under his arms had spread almost all the way down the sides of his shirt. He stared wide-eyed at Oumou from across the road, his mouth hanging open. When he realized that he'd been staring, he quickly turned to avoid all eye contact and hurried in the opposite direction.

Both Vicki and Mrs. Chastaine shook their heads.

"Well, girls," Mrs. Chastaine said, "our stop is right up there. Let's be quick. Good chatting with you, Vicki," she added with a smile. "Take care now." She ushered Oumou and Amanda along and into the store.

Hot pink walls and loud upbeat music assaulted Oumou's sense on two fronts. Her pulse quickened. The harsh twanging in the song made her skin crawl, and the man's voice did nothing to help.

Women sat under hair dryers, reading magazines or chatting with their neighbor. A squat woman with bleach-blonde hair and excessive amounts of makeup bounded from the back, past racks of clothes, cosmetics, and hair products alike.

"Elizabeth!" The woman heaved her chest forward, wrapping Mrs. Chastaine into a hug that Oumou thought would snap the woman in half. "How have you been, darling? I haven't seen you in weeks! Oh, you really should let me do something with that—"

The woman looked down and saw Oumou, and a great smile broke out across her moon-shaped face. "Oh my! Aren't you just the cutest thing?" She looked back at Mrs. Chastaine. "I didn't realize you were adopting!"

"No, Teri, it's not—"

The woman forced herself to bend over, and Oumou wondered if she'd be able to straighten back up. "What's your name, little darling?"

"Oumou." Oumou wilted under the woman's exuberant energy.

"Oumou?" She drew out the word on both ends and seemed positively pleased with the introduction. "I'm Ms. Chambers, but please, call me Teri."

"Okay," Oumou said, still looking at the ground. "Teri."

"Teri, we didn't adopt her" — Mrs. Chastaine sighed — "we found her," she whispered. "I just came to get her some clothes."

"Oh, well why didn't you say so? Right this way, I have the perfect things! And at the perfect price too!" She winked at Oumou.

Mrs. Chastaine rolled her eyes, then smiled down at Oumou. "She's a bit much, but she means well." She followed the woman to the back of the store with Oumou and Amanda in tow.

Oumou nodded. "A bit much."

"Oh, by the way, Elizabeth, have you heard? Sylvia Windsor's granddaughter, the one that went to New York, is pregnant." Teri led them through racks of clothing in the back of the store, plucking off items here and there.

"Oh, that's wonderful, I'm sure Sylvia's elated."

"No, she's devastated. Apparently, the father's" — she glanced down at Oumou sheepishly — "well, Sylvia doesn't approve. Heard she was talking with Reverend Rhodes about it. You'd think the woman was in mourning."

Mrs. Chastaine nodded her head slowly, casting a concerned look down to the two children at her side. Teri got the hint, dropping the subject and returning to shuffling through the various racks of clothing.

"Do you like pink, Oumou?" Teri asked.

"No."

An hour later and they'd finally narrowed it down to three outfits. Two plain casual rompers, and a dress that Mrs. Chastaine deemed suitable for Sunday service, "in case she was here that long."

* * *

Mr. Chastaine emerged from his office scowling as they entered the house, the cord to his desk phone stretched to its limit. "I don't know what else to tell you, Dave, we found a girl in the vineyard." Seeing them back in the house, he lowered his voice. "She has to be somebody's."

"I know nobody said anything about a missing" — his tone dropped to a whisper — "black girl, okay, nobody ever does... Of course it's a race thing!" He gave an apologetic look in response to Mrs. Chastaine's frown. "You know what, just keep looking, okay?" He stormed into his office and slammed the phone into its cradle. With a sigh he slumped onto the living room couch. "Oumou, now that you're feeling better, do you know anybody who we can call to come get you?"

Oumou shook her head.

"Do you know where your mom or your dad are?"

"I don't have a family anymore."

"So...you're an orphan?"

Mrs. Chastaine winced at the bluntness of the question. "Harold."

"Sorry, I just—"

"I'm an experiment," Oumou said flatly. Tears began to well up in her eyes. She felt like something was clamping down on her heart, quickening the pulse and making every beat excruciating. "Please don't make me go back," she whimpered. "I can't..." Her breath caught in her chest, crushed under the same pressure as her heart. She gasped for air. "I can't. I can't."

"Breathe," Harold said, kneeling in front of her. He placed his hands firmly on her shoulders. "In for four, now hold...hold...and breathe out," he said. "Now, again."

Oumou felt her panic begin to dissipate, and the tears that clung to the corners of her eyes ran freely down her cheeks. "I don't want to go back," she said finally.

"It's okay," Mrs. Chastaine said, "you can stay here with us for a while. Until we can figure out a better plan, right?"

Mr. Chastaine raised a single eyebrow at his wife. "Was I going to be consulted on this decision?" he said with a chuckle.

"I knew you'd say yes," his wife said.

"Call the *Enquirer*," he said. "I married a psychic."

The two of them began to laugh and Oumou found herself chuckling as well as she wiped the tears from her eyes. She didn't understand the joke, but the adults' laughter was infectious.

"Thank you," she said quietly. Neither of the adults heard her, and she was glad for that. The moment was nice, and she didn't want to ruin it.

CHAPTER 5

"I HOPE YOU don't plan on interfering." The man next to Leslie hadn't spoken at all when they boarded, and now, thirty minutes into their shared flight, these were the first words out of his mouth.

"Excuse me?" Leslie, in turn, openly acknowledged the man for the first time, turning in his seat to face him.

The man was like a vulture. Beady eyes set deep in a sallow face atop a crooked neck that craned no matter how the man turned. Two rows of perfect teeth grinned at Leslie from a mouth stretched uncomfortably wide: a rictus grin that didn't move when the man spoke. His grey suit hung limp over an emaciated frame, but Leslie swore the body beneath the fabric pulsed and writhed despite the man's stillness. *That ain't right,* he thought, not taking his eyes off the undulations beneath the man's clothes.

"I said, I hope you don't plan on interfering." The wet voice seemed to slop out of the man's mouth like vomit.

Leslie looked around to see if anyone else noticed the odd exchange but found the plane empty save him and the man. Fear prickled at the nape of his neck.

"What don't you want me interfering with?" Leslie tried to get up but found himself stuck. He struggled against the invisible force for a few minutes before giving up and going limp in the tiny airplane seat.

"Archwood." The man rolled his head forward as the word exited his mouth like nails on a chalkboard. He laughed as Leslie gaped in shock. His bird-like eyes didn't blink once as he stared. "The girl."

"Yeah, real funny," Leslie said, trying to retain a portion of his calm. He felt around his leg for the knife he kept in his pocket but found that it wasn't there. *This is wrong.*

Black fluid began to build up around the base of the man's eyes, running down his face and into his grinning mouth, staining his teeth black. The liquid flooded out of his eyes, now just swirling black pits, and onto his suit. The writhing beneath the fabric grew in intensity, as the man's body was wracked with violent spasms. Veins in his face bulged until they burst, causing red blooms to expand under the skin still visible beneath the deluge of black.

Leslie screamed and struggled against the invisible force that held him to his seat. "This isn't real," he shouted. "This isn't real!"

"Isn't it?" the man gurgled. "Feels real to me. Hurts real bad."

The man's head was swelling and turning a deep red. All Leslie could do was watch until, with a sickening pop, the man's head exploded, spraying Leslie in a combination of red and black and bits of skull and brain matter.

Leslie bolted awake in his seat and immediately vomited on the tray in front of him. He snapped his head to his left and saw, not the man from his dream, but a man in a labcoat, with a burn that covered a large portion of the right side of his face. The man stared at Leslie with an inscrutable look before turning his attention back out the window.

"Sir?"

Leslie jumped in his seat again. "Fuck," he said, "what?" He looked up into the face of a frightened stewardess.

"Sir, I'm going to have to ask you to calm down, you're scaring the other passengers," she said.

Leslie looked around, meeting the glares and looks of fear of those around him with his own look of confusion and embarrassed rage.

"Sir, are you all right?" The stewardess put a hand on his shoulder, snapping Leslie's attention back to her. She let out a small squeak and jerked away.

"Yeah," he said, adjusting himself in his seat. "Night terror." He cleared his throat and flashed an unconvincing smile. "It won't happen again."

"It better not, nigger," a voice shouted from the back.

Leslie spun to confront it, but the other passengers refused to meet his eye. He looked around for anyone that looked like him, who would stand with him, but the few that were present avoided his gaze as well.

"Yeah, well, fuck all of you," he mumbled as he slid back into his seat. *Can't blame them though, with me acting like a psycho out of nowhere like that.* He dragged a hand over his face and took a long pull from the flask in his coat pocket. Visions only came while he slept, and he didn't remember falling asleep. He'd just handed the stewardess his coffee and then...whatever it was hadn't felt like a dream. It was too solid, too real. Dreams felt like getting dragged along by a rushing river. But then, he remembered the man's swirling black eyes — what was he supposed to make of it all? The dream was trying to scare him away from whatever was in Archwood. Leslie hated to admit that it might work.

Bravery is not what kept him from boarding another plane immediately after landing; hunger did that. And after a meal and some liquid courage at the Raleigh Airport, reason and his journalistic mind began to reassert themselves. *It had to be a dream,* he thought. *From stress or lack of sleep.*

It took a good hour to get a cabbie to even acknowledge him, but even that didn't dissuade him from his path. He knew the cab would overcharge him, but by the time he climbed in, he didn't have the patience to wait for a friendlier ride. The fare was agreed upon and directions given.

Please don't let this be a bad idea.

* * *

This is the kind of bar a black man wouldn't be caught dead in. Unless, Leslie thought, *he were caught in it. Then he very well might end up dead.* He silently cursed the cabbie for dropping him here in the middle of the night. *Shouldn't have trusted his ass anyway.*

Bracing himself, he put on his best confused negro face, stowed his camera, and stepped through the doors of the Dog-Water Bar. Immediately the rancid smell of hot, day-old beer, sweat, and tobacco filled his lungs. *Lovely*, he thought.

By both the decor and the manner in which the patrons dressed, Leslie could tell the bar was a hotspot for truckers. Mullets and baseball caps adorned the heads of most of the men and a fair amount of the women, while a myriad of country music artists stared down on him from the walls. *Just don't make eye contact with anyone and maybe this will only hurt a little.*

The bartender was a gangly man with dirty blonde hair. Unlike many of the patrons, he had an air of self-respect about him. He gave Leslie a pitying smile, but his eyes said "leave."

"Look," Leslie said, sliding a twenty-dollar bill across the bar, not even bothering to take a seat, "I'm gonna level with you. I don't want to be here, and no one here wants me to be here either. I just need to phone a cab to pick me up and I'll be out of your hair, cool?"

"Yeah, no problem." The boy was trying to pitch his voice down to sound older, but he couldn't have been more than seventeen. Which meant it wasn't his bar. Which meant *when* shit went down, he'd be no help to Leslie. "Phone's in the back," he said, jamming a thumb over his shoulder.

"Thanks, kid," Leslie said, turning away from the bar and bumping right into a mullet that had previously been seated at a table near the entrance.

Fuck.

"Dennis, is the blackie bothering you?" A life of smoking and drinking, both recently, hung about him in a haze Leslie could taste as much as he could smell. He coughed involuntarily at the assault on his senses.

And he's drunk. Double fuck.

"No, Randy, he's okay. No trouble, please," Dennis said, walking around the bar and attempting to come between the two of them. Randy pushed him aside with ease.

"I think he *wants* trouble, striding in here like he owns the place." The man slurred just about every word that came out of his mouth. It barely sounded like English anymore.

"If I did, I'd change the decor and only allow better looking clientele." The words were out of Leslie's mouth before his brain could catch up and veto them. He saw Randy's face darken and knew this was going to be more than a little painful. *You made your bed, Leslie, time to tuck yourself the fuck in.*

"What'd you say?"

"I mean, I've heard of white trash but...I think y'all are taking it a bit too literally." He forced himself to laugh. The bartender stared at him like he'd lost his mind. By now a crowd had gathered, pushing him back against the bar. "When was the last time anyone in this place showered?" Leslie knew the hit was coming, but he didn't know when.

Randy let out an animalistic roar and swung his fist wide for a haymaker to Leslie's face. Leslie closed his eyes and shielded his face with his hands as best he could.

But the blow never came. He peeked through his fingers and saw that Randy was still poised to swing but hadn't. Leslie lowered his hands even more and saw that Randy *couldn't*. Another hand had grabbed him by the wrist.

Randy looked just as shocked as Leslie that his face hadn't been turned into an indistinguishable mess of blood and teeth. He wrenched around in the grip to face the unknown interloper. Leslie saw a face with a burn on it, and a cold, empty smile. *The man from the plane?* A chill ran down his spine. The man with the burned face had eyes just like the man in Leslie's dream: inky black pits that leaked a dark substance, like he was always crying. The pitiless holes bored into Randy like obsidian drills.

"The hell are you?" the biker slurred. If he noticed the man's ocular issue, he did a fair job of hiding his fear behind drunk bravado. "What's wrong with your eyes?"

So he did notice, Leslie thought.

The eyeless man with the half-burned face contorted his countenance into an uneven scowl. With a monotonous, snake-like voice, he said, "I am not here for you."

The sentence made Leslie's hairs stand on end.

"You should've stayed out of this, scar face." Randy tried to wrench his arm free of the other man's grasp to no avail. "The fuck?"

"No." The man's scowl cracked into a shark-toothed smile that made Leslie's stomach cramp with fear. "This is what I want."

"Gentleman, please," Dennis tried to interject, "no fighting inside. How about a round of drinks on the house?" The fear coming off him was palpable. His throat bobbed as he swallowed hard, trying to keep his nerve.

Something in Randy's liquor-addled mind must have been sending the right signals, because for a second the tough guy bravado faltered. In the next second it was back, but he still backed down. "Yeah," he said, jerking his fist away with success this time, before turning back to the bar, "drinks."

He didn't see what Leslie saw. The burn-faced man's shadow moved, spreading out like vines snaking across the ground. The individual tendrils slithered along the wood panel floor before detaching and rearing up like threatening cobras. Leslie wanted to warn the man, but it was too late. The first tendril pierced right through his thigh. A thick geyser of blood from the femoral artery sprayed onto the floor. Randy went down to one knee and looked into Leslie's eyes with a pained grimace. He knew how long he didn't have, and so did Leslie.

"You son of a bitch," Randy roared, wheeling around on an unsteady leg and throwing a surprise uppercut from his kneeling position. He missed. His meat-hammer fist whizzed past the eyeless man's face and sent Randy toppling to the floor. He clutched at his leg still pulsing bright crimson with every beat of his heart.

A collective rustling of weapons being drawn, and knuckles cracking filled the bar. *This number,* Leslie thought, *is my cue to become scarce.* The entrance to the bar was past the shadow man and a crowd of more than pissed off rednecks. He didn't like his odds of making it out through that gauntlet.

Leslie didn't know which person in the crowd fired the shot that set the massacre into motion, and he didn't stay to find out. As the mob surged toward the burned man, Leslie ducked down low and half crawled back behind the bar and hunkered down in the space between two large kegs. The smell of stale beer and expired meat was suffocating, but he choked it down and tucked himself away tight. With any luck, no one saw him escape in the chaos. He hoped.

Leslie heard Dennis start to say something. His voice broke into a too-short scream followed by a moist puncturing sound. Leslie heard the suction as one of those tendrils pulled itself out of what he could only imagine was another gaping wound.

The bar spiraled into a riot of violence and noise after that. Stray bullets shattered bottles of alcohol older than Leslie, embedding themselves in solid wood walls or pinging off the décor only to ricochet somewhere else. One such bullet embedded itself in the keg to Leslie's left, eliciting a harsh gasp from the man as warm beer piddled onto his pants. The sound of a bone snapping cracked overtop the rest of the noise. No scream followed. Leslie didn't want to think of why. Leslie retched as a thick, coppery smell began to permeate the air, smothering the smell of beer and smoke. Blood splattered across the back wall behind the bar and Leslie urged himself deeper between the two kegs. It had been a while since he prayed, but he figured right now was a damn good time to start again.

Eventually the cacophony began to settle. All Leslie heard was the slithering sound of those black tendrils, now drenched with blood, snaking their way across the floor. From that, Leslie knew the bargoers were dead. All of them. He looked at his watch. Not even five minutes. Finally, complete silence fell over the bar. A morbid thought crossed Leslie's mind: *silent as the grave.*

* * *

Leslie didn't know how long he waited in the silence, but even when he finally decided to peer over the top of the bar, it didn't seem like long enough. And it wasn't. Leslie's head had barely crested the top of the bar when a harsh voice made him cry out and curse.

"I know you're there," the man with the burned face said. "Stand up, Leslie Johnson."

The sound of his own name said in that icy whisper made Leslie's flesh crawl. He rose to his feet and realized that his whole body was trembling. As he came eye level with the man, he saw the thorny tendrils slither their way up into the sleeves of the man's blood-stained labcoat. Black tears poured from eyeless sockets that seemed to track Leslie as he walked around to the front of the bar.

Leslie kept his eyes on the man, desperately trying to ignore the acrid smell of blood that hung like a fog in the air. He almost slipped in something slick, and his heart began to riot in his chest. He finally took in the rest of the room.

The bargoers' bodies lay strewn all about the bar, and to Leslie's horror, he realized that he couldn't count even one that remained completely intact. Limbs, heads, and less distinguishable bloody shreds were piled up haphazardly at the eyeless man's feet. Leslie gasped, and immediately choked on the metallic taste in the air. It clung to his tongue as he swallowed his rising gorge. His stomach tightened into a knot, and he willed himself not to vomit. He could taste the bile burning at the back of his throat as he tried to speak.

"You got a name?" he asked. He tried to act unphased, but his voice faltered as he spoke.

"I have been called the King of Thorns," the man replied.

"That's more of a title than a name," Leslie said. His nervousness set his mouth running, and he hoped to God it wouldn't get him killed.

"My name is lost to time."

"Is the burn on your face—"

"This body is just like the clothes on your back."

"Right... Look," Leslie said, "I am *this* close to pissing myself, so I've got to know. Are you going to kill me or not? Because if not, I would rather be anywhere but here."

The King of Thorns frowned, creasing the skin around his burn and casting his entire face in shadows. Leslie thought that for a moment a flame sparked deep in the darkness of those inky black pits that replaced his eyes. "It was I who tormented the Christ when he descended into Hell." Tendrils lashed out from his sleeves, crushing through the bar and spraying Leslie with debris.

"Fuck. Okay," Leslie shouted, jumping away from the counter. "The plane," he said, trying unsuccessfully to keep his eyes locked on the other man. "You were there too. And now... Oh God." He caught sight of Randy's lifeless eyes staring up at him from a pool of his own blood and heaved.

"Yes, I was," the King of Thorns said. "You have a fragment of power, and I used it to my own ends." He retracted his vines and grimaced as he took hold of his right hand, gazing at it with something Leslie recognized as fury.

"But you spoke to me. That doesn't happen in my visions." Leslie's foot bumped against an arm that looked like it might have once been the bartender's. He froze as it did, before taking a shaking step around it.

"Why shouldn't I speak to you? After all, you were looking through my eyes." His manner of speaking was different than before, less unhinged and far more imperious. "Unfit though you are."

"How's that?"

"You have little more than a fraction of my power. A touch of dark magic. And you use it simply to watch. Your inaction disgusts me."

"Magic?" Leslie bit back the sarcastic reply that his brain immediately offered up. "On the plane, you mentioned a girl—"

He was cut off by an abysmal moan emanating from the man's gaping mouth. The black tendrils thrashed about him, breaking tables, chairs, and anything else that got in their way. Leslie flinched behind his arms, stumbled back towards the bar, and strongly considered returning to his hiding place.

"She is mine," the King of Thorns hissed.

Leslie's throat turned to ash, and he coughed as he tried to continue speaking. "Got it," he said. "But what do you want her for?"

A cruel smile distorted the King of Thorns' scarred face. "For too long I have been stuck like you as punishment for my actions. Trapped between Heaven and Hell, watching as the world continued on." He spat on a nearby corpse. "As *you* continued on."

"But then," he continued, "I was given a blessing. Your kind, fools that you are, opened a portal to my prison and let me out, but not only that, you presented me with the perfect host as well."

"A host?" Leslie said. "Like the man you're...wearing...right now?"

"Your bodies tether me to this world and keep me from being pulled back to the void, but look." He raised a hand, turning it to and fro. The flesh on his hand was melting off, dripping down his skeletal remains like wax from a burning candle.

"That's disgusting," Leslie said, looking away.

"I burn through you like kindling." The King of Thorns grabbed at the melting flesh and ripped it free, tossing the clump to the floor. Another dead lump of flesh in a makeshift slaughterhouse.

"And you're going to do that to me?" Leslie choked down the lump in his throat.

The King of Thorns laughed. "No, not you."

"The girl?"

"The girl."

"The girl is different?"

"With her power, I could shrug off the decay and exist in this space forever."

"As one of us?" Leslie asked, hopefully.

"As your master."

Shocking, Leslie thought bitterly. "Right." He took a deep breath. Fear still clawed at his heart like a wild animal, but he fought it back. *Ask the next question,* he thought, *just ask the next question.* The mantra had gotten him through some of the worst scenarios in his life. He repeated it to himself before asking, "Why tell me all this?" His stomach dropped. "You're going to kill me..."

"No," the King of Thorns said, teeth bared. "After all, every master needs a slave."

Leslie felt a burning spike of rage pulse at the core of his chest, stomping down on his fear. He clenched his fists until the nails dug deep into his palms.

The King of Thorns stepped closer. Leslie tried to back away but bumped into the bar. There was nowhere to go. He grabbed Leslie's face in bloodstained hands. "You're all so easy to kill." He smiled at him. "Stay out of my way, good and faithful servant, or I'll spend a millennium removing the first layer of your skin, and then I'll start on the next one. Clear?"

Leslie locked eyes with the man, clenched his jaw, and growled, "Crystal."

"Wonderful," he said.

There was a gust of wind, and the entire bar plunged into complete darkness. When the lights came back on, the King of Thorns was gone. Leslie stood alone in the bar, surrounded by disemboweled and dismembered corpses. He felt numb. His body barely responded to the whirling storm of emotions that wracked his mind. Finally, a single, logical thought pushed its way to the surface. *I can't stay here.* It was enough to get him moving. He searched around and found the back office of the bar. Pinned to the wall was an old map of the surrounding area. The bar sat in the middle of nowhere, surrounded on all sides by a deciduous forest. Archwood was on the other side of that forest. Too far to walk at night. He scanned the map more and found a small clearing with an X marked over a cabin in its center, about halfway between the bar and the town. The word "blacks" was scrawled in an angry red beneath the cabin.

"For once, racists are useful," Leslie said. "First time for everything, I guess."

It wouldn't be pleasant, but he could make it. He stuffed the map in his back pocket, pulled a long swig from an unbroken bottle of whiskey, thought for a second about putting it back, said, "Fuck that," and stuffed it in his largest jacket pocket. He let himself out the back door, just in case anyone else showed up. His mind raced as he entered the dark cluster of trees that crept up to the back entrance of the bar.

* * *

The forest between the bar and the city stretched on forever. It was late. Every tree was a monster reaching out to grab him, and every noise brought his death that much closer.

"This was a terrible *fucking* idea," Leslie said. He didn't care about the cold rain soaking his skin or the sucking mud beneath his feet. The branches scratching at his face barely phased him, and he only stopped running the few times he tripped. Bruises and scrapes screamed for acknowledgement, but Leslie knew there was worse pain behind him.

Sometime after his escape, the police had found the bar; he'd heard the K-9 units and knew they'd be on him quick. Now the pulsing flash of their car lights bathed the forest behind him, and flashlights scanned the forest floor. Every now and then he could catch snippets of shouts or the braying howl of a police dog. Whenever the brush rustled, he felt his heart leap into his chest.

You aren't who they want, Leslie thought. *But if they find you, you know damn well you'll be* exactly *who they was looking for.*

The sounds of the cops were faint over the downpour of rain, but he could tell they were getting closer. Too close behind for his comfort. Or his safety.

"Rain is good, though. Dogs can't track as well in rain," he said, wiping the water from his eyes. *Sure, they can't. Probably trained to chase your black ass all the way up the river.*

The trees parted on all sides, giving way to a small clearing. A log cabin rested in the middle of the clearing and looked as though it had been abandoned for a while.

Leslie gasped and laughed with relief. "Thank god."

There were no lights from inside, and no smoke from the chimney. The roof was intact, but the deck was warping down, collapsing under its own weight. No one had been here in a while. Leslie sprinted for the small building, pounding up the creaking porch steps towards the front door.

He didn't hear the police dog until it bounded up the steps behind him. The German Shepherd latched onto his forearm and sunk its teeth deep into the leather of his coat. Leslie screamed before stifling the noise by biting down on his hand.

"Let go of me, you bastard," he growled through teeth and hand, flinging his arm, and the attached dog, around. "Get off!"

"Sheriff, I think Magnum went this way," a voice in the distance shouted.

Leslie looked to see flashlights dancing over trees close to his new hideout. He looked back down at the dog, rumbling in a gentler fashion now, but still not letting go. "Fine, guess you're coming with me, Magnum."

With the dog still thoroughly attached, Leslie tried the door. It opened with no resistance. He dragged the dog into the house, muttering curses and trying to ignore the pain coursing through his arm.

"Place like this, middle of nowhere. Got to have a food storage cellar." He scoured the wooden panel floorboard. He thumped along the wood frantically with his foot until he heard a hollow sound. "Ha!"

A square section of the flooring just barely separated from the rest. Before entering the hiding spot, he crossed the floor and broke the back window of the room and shuffled his feet on the floor to cover the trail he left in the dust. Using his one free arm, he lifted the trapdoor to reveal a set of stairs descending into darkness.

"Hope you're not afraid of the dark," he said, and stepped into the cellar, closing the door behind him. His eyes began adjusting to the lack of light as soon as he closed the door. The cellar smelled of spices, mildew, and fermenting things. The combination was both intoxicating and nauseating. Leslie found that after a few breaths, he felt dizzy.

Magnum released his arm and started barking. Leslie immediately clamped his hands around the dog's mouth, wincing at the pain, and praying it wouldn't wriggle out and tear off his fingers. He sucked air through his teeth and scrunched his eyes tight. The dog's barking became a soft whimper in the dark.

He's a scaredy-cat, Leslie thought. A wave of relief washed over him, leaving only the throbbing in his arm and the sound of the dogs whining in the dark. "You best be quiet. If they find us, they'll shoot through you to get to me, I promise you that," Leslie said, stroking the dog softly with the hand on his injured arm, which prompted it to settle into silence. "I don't want to die, but I really don't want to die with a dog's death on my conscious. So. Stay. Calm." Leslie slowly released the dog's mouth. "And don't you bite me again," he whispered. "Please."

Footsteps tramped overhead, and Leslie's breath caught in his throat. He couldn't make out words well through the rain and sounds of movement, but they hadn't found him yet.

"Magnum!" one of the cops shouted.

The dog twitched and went to bark, but Leslie hushed him with a soothing noise. On a shelf to his left, he saw the distinctive butcher paper that indicated meat. Reaching slowly, he unwrapped the meat, grabbed a piece of jerky, and offered it to the dog, who tore at it greedily and devoured the meat in silence. Magnum licked his lips when he finished and settled down on the floor, crossing his paws and resting his head on them.

Leslie couldn't make out the next words, but they were followed by several pairs of boots pounding out of the house and eventually fading into silence. His trick must have worked. Hearing his owners leave, Magnum began to whimper loudly.

"Here, here," Leslie said. He handed the dog several more pieces of the jerky resting on the shelf. "You were a very good boy."

The dog snatched the meat treat and gnawed it greedily, but never took his eyes off Leslie. Deciding the dog was fully preoccupied for the moment, Leslie inspected the bite wound. The leather kept the dog from turning his arm into meatloaf, but the discoloration from the bruises was already apparent, even in the low light.

"Lucky I like dogs," he muttered, to which Magnum's ears perked up and he offered a defiant grunt.

He pulled the bottle of whiskey from his jacket, surprised it had managed to stay put during his journey, and sat down with his back against the stairs. There was just enough liquid left in the bottle for one swig, by his standards, and he took it down in three gulps. The whiskey's medicinal properties slowly turned the agony in his arm into a dull ache. He rested it across his stomach and watched as the dog watched him from the other end of the room. They passed a while like this until Leslie finally relented. He hadn't really slept since before his flight. Exhaustion dragged his eyelids down and he slept without a dream.

CHAPTER 6

OUMOU LAY IN the bed in the guest room, staring up at the peeling white paint on the ceiling. Across the room, Amanda slept in her own bed. Earlier she'd demanded that her father move the wiry day bed so that she could sleep near Oumou. She didn't want her to feel alone or unwanted. Despite the oddness, Oumou appreciated the gesture.

She could hear the other girl's faint breaths every few seconds. Oumou tried to match the breathing, hoping it would lead her to a similar sleep. The night crept on at a snail's pace. Oumou's stomach growled. She hadn't eaten much for dinner and now the bubbling in her abdomen threatened to keep her up all night.

I could get food, she thought. *No. What if they catch me?*

"They'll be angry," she whispered to herself. "They'll throw me out."

Her stomach growled again, contradicting everything she said.

"I can't," she said.

The gurgling of her stomach grew so loud, she worried it might wake Amanda up.

Would she be angry? she thought. *I should get food, so she won't wake up.*

"Just don't get caught," she mumbled. Slipping out of bed, she padded her way to the kitchen, taking care not to make a sound. She opened the fridge and took stock of the food. Fruit, chicken, tea, bread, cheeses, and a box labeled "Pizza." She rubbed her stomach and took out a smooth green apple. Her mouth began to water.

The lights clicked on.

"Oumou? What are you doing up?" Mrs. Chastaine stood in a white nightgown, rubbing at her eyes.

Oumou went rigid and the apple slipped from her hand. It tumbled to the floor and rolled up against the refrigerator. "I'm so sorry," she said, breathlessly. "I just...I'm so hungry."

Mrs. Chastaine reached down and picked up the apple. She wiped it off on her clothes and inspected it in the light. "Looks fine." She handed it back to Oumou.

"You're not mad?" Oumou asked.

"No, sweetie," Mrs. Chastaine said, "you just startled me is all." She rubbed her eyes. "Woke me up."

"Sorry."

Mrs. Chastaine gave a tired smile and patted Oumou on the head. "Don't worry about it." She yawned. "Did you want me to slice it for you?"

Behind Mrs. Chastaine, standing at the window looking in on the living room, was a man with a scar covering half of his face. He stared at Oumou through two black pits that weren't quite eyes and gave her an unsettling smile. A white coat hung down from his gaunt frame.

Oumou shrieked in fright, then, remembering Amanda, she clamped her hand over her mouth.

Mrs. Chastaine wheeled around. "What is it?" she said, looking directly at the man. She looked back at Oumou. "Did you see something?"

"You don't see...?" Oumou asked. "With the dark eyes?"

Mrs. Chastaine glanced over her shoulder a second time. She sighed and knelt down in front of Oumou. "I know bad people hurt you, but they aren't here. You're safe, and there is no one there."

While Mrs. Chastaine talked, the man in the labcoat continued to stare at Oumou with the same unwavering smile. Black fluid dribbled down his cheeks. *He's crying,* Oumou thought. *While he's smiling...*

"Oumou?" Mrs. Chastaine asked, pulling Oumou's attention back to the woman in front of her. "Did you hear what I said?"

Oumou looked back at the doorway, but the man was gone. "Yes, ma'am, I heard you."

Mrs. Chastaine turned to look at the window. Seeing nothing, she said, "Good. I'm going back to bed. Eat quick so you don't wake Amanda with the light. Don't want her being tired and grumpy, do we?"

"No, ma'am," Oumou said. "I'm gonna eat the apple back in the bedroom if that's okay." She paused for a minute. "Good night."

Mrs. Chastaine smiled. "Good night, Oumou, try to get some sleep. You probably need it." She closed the refrigerator door and turned off the lights, leaving Oumou to stare at the window in the darkness. Oumou watched for a little bit, standing and listening to the sound of her own breathing. Once or twice she saw a shadow flicker outside the glass panes, but the man didn't return.

In my head, she thought. *I'm safe here,* she tried to convince herself. Instead she found herself alone in the dark and afraid. She hurried back to the guest room and checked that Amanda was still asleep. She checked around for the eyeless man, her heart pounding in her chest. She didn't see anything. Relieved, she plopped onto the bed and held the apple in front of her face. *Focus,* she thought. Bending spoons had been an early test, and she'd gotten good at that quickly. *Just like the spoons. Easy.* The apple's green skin quivered and rippled for a second before beginning to peel itself off the apple. It started at the base of the stem and unwound itself all the way down the rest of the apple. The peeled skin floated across the room and slipped into a nearby wastebasket. The apple itself hovered in front of Oumou's furrowed brow. With no ceremony, the apple fell into eight equal slices in a perfect stack on her lap. She felt a small wave of nausea wash over her, and her head began to throb. *Not that easy,* she thought.

"How'd you do that?" Oumou jumped at the sound of Amanda's voice. She hadn't heard the girl sneak over to her bedside. The apple slices toppled over.

"Do what?" Oumou asked, feigning ignorance and covering the apple with her hands. She gulped down a calming breath of air.

"You made the apple float!"

"No, I didn't, you're seeing things," Oumou said. She thought of a believable excuse. "I threw the apple in the air."

"In all those pieces?" Amanda put her hands on her hips, imitating what her mother did when she was upset. "And how'd you get the skin off without a peeler?"

Oumou stared at the traitorous apple pieces peeking through her fingers. "Don't tell your mom or dad, please."

"Why not?" Amanda frowned, hands still on her hips.

"Because...it's a secret," Oumou said. "Between friends. I'm your best friend, right?"

A bright smile spread across Amanda's face. "Yes!" she beamed. "But tomorrow you have to show me some more. Deal?" She extended a lily-white hand, icy blue in the darkness.

Oumou took the hand in her own and mumbled, "Deal."

With that, Oumou rolled over in her bed and pulled the comforter up over her head, spilling the apple slices to the floor. She thought she heard a voice call out to her, but she couldn't make it out from within her cotton fortress. It felt like hours before she finally fell asleep, but eventually she did.

* * *

Is this a dream? Oumou thought as her eyes flicked open. It was still nighttime, but something was wrong. Everything around her drifted in and out of focus, taking on a tinge of surrealism. Objects bent and warped in places where straight edges should have been. The colors in the room all bled into each other, swirling and dancing to a rhythm that made her head spin.

"Hello?" Oumou called. Her voice echoed back to her, first louder, then softer.

The room was the same one she'd fallen asleep in, so far as she could tell. Her blankets that had comforted her as she drifted off clung to her like a straitjacket. She couldn't move. Straining her neck, she looked and saw that Amanda still slept in the next bed over. *Not a dream.* The hairs on her arms stood on end as she felt someone's eyes on her. She scanned the room until she saw him.

Even in the dark of the room the man's eyes were darker still, as if the concept of light didn't exist in their presence. His mouth was drawn out in a mournful scowl. He stared at her silently from the foot of her bed. Splatters of red covered his labcoat. Oumou thought her heart might burst from the pounding in her chest.

Oumou shrunk down into the blankets, trying her best to escape his line of sight. Shadowy tendrils crept around the edges of her vision as she stared at him. She clamped her eyes shut, then opened them again, hoping he'd be gone. He wasn't. The corners of his mouth twitched up into what might have been a smile on anyone else's face. On his, it looked like a threat.

"Who are you?" Oumou said in a hushed voice. Her throat had gone dry.

The man walked around to the side of her bed and reached out a hand towards her. Oumou's panic mounted as five skeletal fingers barely strung together by tendons and oozing flesh came into view.

"What do you want?" Oumou tried to shift out of his reach, willing herself to get out of the bed, but whatever held her in place refused to let her go. "Get away from me!" She felt the heat radiating off his fingers as they drew closer to her face. "Amanda," Oumou screamed, desperate for help. "Amanda!"

The man paused and cocked his head at her. "She can't hear you." He sounded as if he was choking on each word. Oumou wished she could cover her ears to block out the sound. "Nor could she save you if she did." His cruel smile returned. "Tonight, you're all mine." What looked like thorny vines wriggled their way out of his sleeves and onto her bed. They snaked their way up the sheets towards her face. She felt them stinging around her eyes and mouth.

"Get off of me!" Oumou shouted. A rush went out of her, blowing the vines away and obliterating the man's skeletal arm. He jerked what remained of the shattered bones away with a hiss.

The man nursed the wound with his good arm, but as Oumou watched, the flesh on that one began to melt away as well. He snapped his head back at her and she saw his face. Where the burn once had been now dripped away, revealing the muscles and skull behind his face. His teeth ground together, and a wet ragged sound escaped the now gaping hole as he spoke. "No! So much power. I'm so close." He tried to extend his vines once more, but they writhed and evaporated into black smoke. "So. Close." He let out a pained gasp. "You're too strong to take like this. I need a new..." He turned his head to Amanda, then back to Oumou. "She's lucky you'd defend her," he said, and his body melted into a puddle on the floor that quickly evaporated into steam, leaving nothing in its wake.

Oumou watched a shadow, all the darker in the blue moonlight, slither up the wall and disappear at the window with a furious hiss. Instantly the tension in the room vanished, and Oumou found she could move freely beneath her sheets. She gasped out a weak sob and buried her head beneath the comforter.

Finally, she peeked her head out, half expecting the man to be there watching her once more. The room was dark and still. She heard Amanda's soft snores from the other side of the room. She looked at the bedside table. The clock blinked a digital red 3:15 AM.

Oumou sunk into the blankets with a heavy sigh. Her eyelids felt heavy, but her mind was racing. *He's gone*, she tried to convince herself, but she couldn't shake the image of the shadow slithering out of her window. *I'm not safe*. The image of his blood-stained white coat flashed in her mind. It came with other memories. Needles. Scalpels. Electric shocks. Her breathing grew rapid and uneven. She felt her chest tighten around burning lungs. *No*, she thought, *he left. I fought back, and he left*. She looked over herself, eyes flicking over the shadows on her dark skin. *I'm not hurt*. She closed her eyes and tried to calm herself the way Mr. Chastaine had shown her. *In for four. Hold. Hold. Hold. Now breathe*. She repeated the exercise until her pulse slowed to its normal rate.

Amanda snorted softly and rolled in her bed. Oumou looked over at her and remembered what the eyeless man had said. She'd protected Amanda. Made her safe. Oumou felt the tinge of a smile on her face. It felt foreign, but still familiar.

"We're safe," she said. She rolled over and pulled the blankets up to her neck. She remembered seeing the clock transition to 3:30, and after that nothing. Just a warm and peaceful darkness.

* * *

Oumou woke with a shriek as Amanda pounced on her bed to wake her up. She panicked and lashed out, knocking the blonde girl off the bed with an invisible force. Amanda landed on the floor with a surprised gasp. Her face was a mask of confusion. She stared up at Oumou with her mouth open.

Oumou started to apologize, but Amanda cut her off.

"That was fun," she said, clambering back onto the bed and giving Oumou an expectant look. "Do it again."

"Do what again?" Mrs. Chastaine stepped into the room and gave both girls a questioning look. "It sounded like someone fell."

Oumou's eyes widened. "No, I—"

"She was juggling, and I scared her, because I got so excited," Amanda lied. Not missing a beat, she held up three dolls Oumou hadn't seen her take from the dollhouse.

Oumou couldn't help but give the other girl a perplexed look. Amanda's bright smile didn't falter one bit. Oumou turned to Mrs. Chastaine with a less-than-convincing smile and said, "That's right."

"Oh, that's neat, where'd you learn to do that?" Mrs. Chastaine smiled at Oumou with genuine curiosity.

"I, uh...didn't have a lot to do...in the lab." Oumou gave a sad smile back, hoping Mrs. Chastaine wouldn't see through the lie. The white coats had never given her any real time to herself except to sleep, and even then, she could feel them watching her. She clamped her mouth shut after she finished, not trusting it to follow through with the lie. Her throat was already tightening up. She couldn't juggle and didn't even know what it was.

"Oh," Mrs. Chastaine said, changing the subject, "well, breakfast is ready, you two. Come on down." She left the door open and retreated back down to the house's main level.

Amanda was the first off the bed and was out of the room before Oumou could even react. The boundless energy of the other girl made a genuine warmth spark in her heart. Her smile felt a little less sad. Oumou slid out of the sheets, placed Amanda's dolls back in the dollhouse, and followed the girl down the steps.

* * *

Oumou had never seen so much food on one table. Pancakes, eggs, sausage, bacon, fruit, toast, orange juice, and milk. The combination of delicious smells threatened to overwhelm her, and before she knew it, her mouth had filled to the brim with saliva in anticipation of the meal. Her plate, which she unabashedly piled high with multiple portions of everything, was soon emptied, and Oumou sat back in her chair and let out a belch of contentment. She stared sheepishly at the wide-eyed family around the table.

"That was delicious," she mumbled.

"Well, her appetite sure is healthy." Mr. Chastaine laughed as he cut his second pancake into smaller pieces.

"I'm glad you liked it," Mrs. Chastaine said with a smile. "There's plenty to go around, so help yourself." She pointed out that a few remnants of the hasty meal lingered on Oumou's face and handed her a napkin. Oumou's face warmed in embarrassment, until she saw that Amanda followed her example and wolfed down an equally massive amount of food.

The three Chastaines sat around the table, eating and talking, and occasionally pulling Oumou into their conversations. She found herself wondering if this is what every family was like. *Is this what I could've had?*

Amanda's voice broke her from her reverie. "Mom, can Oumou and I go out to the vineyard to play?"

"Sweetie," her mother said. "It's Sunday, you know we have to go to church."

CHAPTER 7

OUMOU SHIFTED UNCOMFORTABLY in her dress. Mrs. Chastaine called it her "Sunday best." Oumou thought it was the worst. Tight, itchy, and hot. She was already sweating through the thick fabric.

She gave a pleading look to Mr. Chastaine in his khaki pants and polo shirt, but he simply shrugged. He'd been trying all morning to convince his wife not to go on account of Oumou. All he'd succeeded in doing was making the woman angry. Resigned, he switched on the radio. A man's creaking voice warbled out of the static-filled speaker. Oumou winced as he tried to hit a note out of his range.

"I don't want to go." Oumou's voice was still hoarse from all her screaming last night. Speaking didn't feel pleasant on her throat. "Bad people."

"Now, Oumou, Sunday is God's day, and God wants everyone to go to church," Mrs. Chastaine said, kneeling down to adjust Oumou's dress. She brushed off some lint and gave the girl's hair a conflicted look. "Besides, churches are safe spaces. They bring people comfort."

"Yeah, Oumou, no one's ever done anything bad in the name of God," Mr. Chastaine said, rolling his eyes. "Not like the Crusades, the Inquisition, or—"

Mrs. Chastaine rounded on her husband. "Harold!"

"Sorry, honey, but I'm with Oumou on this one. I don't think it's a good idea. People in this town are a little sensitive about...well, you know."

Mrs. Chastaine's eyes narrowed, and she pointed an accusatory finger at her husband. She flung down the pair of slender white gloves. "The people in this town are good people. I think we're all beyond things like racism now." She paused. "We've been here for almost two years and never once had a problem."

"Yeah, but—"

She waved him down and turned to Oumou. "It'll be all right, okay? God's watching out for you. He's always protecting us."

Oumou looked away. *Then where was he when I needed him?*

"Now," Mrs. Chastaine said, flipping a stray hair from her face. "Are we ready?"

Amanda sat on the couch, her face smeared with a dark chocolate that clashed horribly with the pristine white of her dress. She unwrapped another Hershey's Kiss, placing it into her mouth and savoring it like it was the first and last bit of chocolate she'd ever have. "I don't think so," she said.

Her mother sighed and fussed over the young girl's face, scrubbing it with a wet cloth until her cheeks shined a bright cheery pink.

"All right, let's go," Mrs. Chastaine said, heading towards the door.

As she stepped across the threshold, a cramping nausea settled like stones in the pit of Oumou's stomach.

* * *

Leslie woke to the warm, moist smell of dog-breath on his face. A slobber-covered tongue dragged its way up and down his face, leaving a trail of slime in its wake.

"Bah." He wiped his face and sat up. "None of that."

Magnum barked indignantly.

"Need I remind you of this," Leslie said, holding up his wounded arm. "Your handiwork."

He stood, wiping the cobwebs from his slacks and dusting off his blazer. The food cellar had not made for the ideal resting spot. Quite the opposite. The chill had seeped into his bones, making his joints ache, and he had a crick in his neck that no amount of stretching and kneading could work out. There was nothing in the cellar that any human would consider decent to eat. His stomach groaned. It'd been a full day since he'd eaten, but almost everything down here was rotten. The last of the jerky had gone to pacifying Magnum last night.

"Bar's the closest thing," he said to the dog. "Probably still some fresh food in the back. But you know what they say about returning to the scene of a crime."

He flung open the cellar door and stepped into the dim light of the cabin. With the light, he could better appreciate the interior. All of the furniture was handmade from strong, dark wood. The floor panels were meticulously ordered and uncannily same in sizing. Electric lights were spread throughout the house. Leslie flicked the nearest light switch. A low buzz reverberated through the house before the electric pop of a lightbulb signaled its end. Sparks fell to the floor, catching quickly on the layer of dust. Leslie hurried to stamp them out. He flicked the switch off.

"Can't burn down the hideout," he muttered.

Leslie drifted aimlessly through the house, trying to ignore his furious stomach, until his eyes caught on something hanging on the wall in the kitchen. It was a picture of a black family. A woman with natural hair held a young girl in her hands as she stood next to a man in a military uniform. Both of them beamed out at him from the shattered glass inside the frame.

"Poor bastards," Leslie said, remembering the angry scrawl on the map from the bar. "Rest in power." He pictured the rest of the map in his mind. There was a path on the north side of the clearing that would lead him straight into town. "Well, I guess it's time for me to go see what all this is about. Think they'll offer me breakfast?" He pulled on his trenchcoat and watched as Magnum padded over to the door. "Oh no, you're staying here." He opened the cellar door, snatched up his camera, and pointed at the stairs. "Go."

Magnum began scratching at the front door of the cabin and let out a series of echoing barks. The dog spun in circles and then began to howl.

"Hush now," Leslie hissed. "You're gonna bring everyone right to our doorstep."

The dog barked, scratched, and howled until, with a heavy sigh, Leslie opened the door and said, "Let's go."

Magnum trotted outside and turned back to look at him expectantly.

"Somehow, I feel like you took *me* prisoner, and not the other way around." Leslie reached down and begrudgingly rubbed the dog's head. "Come on, mutt."

The dirt path wound through the forest. With the sun out, the trees were less scary. Vibrant green leaves showing the beginning signs of changing were tipped in yellow and orange. Leslie stopped and took a moment to appreciate the beauty around him until his stomach began its complaining once more. He walked in silence, watching as every now and then Magnum would bolt off, terrifying some squirrel or deer with a rapid-fire stream of barks, only for him to come back looking dejected when the other creature would frantically scurry off into the distance.

"You're too loud," Leslie said dryly. "Sneak if you want to catch one."

It wasn't long before the trees began to thin, and Leslie could make out the shape of a small town in the distance. He stopped as the forest ended and gave way to at least an acre of brilliant green vineyard. The vines were rich and ripe with bronze-green grapes draped over fence posts and hanging low to the ground. His stomach cried out to be filled. He rushed between the rows of vines, sliding to a stop on his knees. He plucked a bunch from the vines, his eyes searching for anyone who looked like they might own the place. Seeing no one, he gorged himself on several of the juicy orbs as he looked out towards the town. People were all flocking to a great black building near the center of the town. Leslie looked at his watch.

"Guess it is that time, eh, boy?" he said, giving the dog an absent-minded head scratch. "Folks got to get their Jesus on. What say you and I go take a gander?"

Magnum gave a hearty bark and began sprinting towards the town.

Leslie let out a breathy curse and set off at a leisurely pace down the curve of the hill.

* * *

The church's spires pierced the sky and glared down at Oumou as they approached the obsidian-colored building. She couldn't help but notice how out of place the structure seemed. While the homes and stores looked relatively new, Oumou thought the church looked like it had been in that exact same spot forever. As they got closer, she realized that the stone was not actually black. Bits of grey peeked out from behind the black char of a long-ago fire. It had a presence that made Oumou shudder. The knot in her stomach squeezed tighter, forcing bile up to the back of her throat as the heavy wooden doors came into view.

The doors were held open by thick iron chains. People filed into the building ahead of them. Oumou recognized Teri the hairdresser, Vicki the librarian, and Leah Buckett and her husband. Each of them stopped to greet a man in black jeans and a black button-down. A white collar pressed into his neck, making it look like he was staring down his nose at everyone who approached him. She heard his voice, booming and melodic over the hum of the small crowd.

"Ah, Teri, you finally return to us. I see you're no longer ill," he said, drawing the rotund woman into a hug. "Welcome back." Oumou couldn't help but notice how uncomfortable he looked with her in his arms. Amanda had never looked uncomfortable when she hugged Oumou.

"Oh, thank you kindly, reverend," Teri said boisterously, practically vibrating with energy as usual. She pulled away from his grip with a smile and slid past him into the darkness of the church. "God is good," she called back.

"Yes," the man in black said, turning his back to her and once again facing the arriving worshippers. His smile was plastered on his face as his eyes scanned the face of each and every entrant, shaking hands and giving awkward embraces. Oumou shrunk away as his eyes fell on her with a cold appraisal, the smile dropping away from his face.

As they got closer to the entrance, the knot in Oumou's stomach became downright painful. She clutched her stomach and did everything in her power to keep from doubling over. By the time they reached the man in black, she thought she might puke on his perfect black shoes. She clamped her mouth shut and willed the urge back down her throat. Her stomach gurgled in protest.

"Harold, Elizabeth, sweet little Amanda, and...you're new." The man looked down his nose at Oumou, looking her up and down as though he was appraising her worth. He appeared to find it lacking.

"Oumou, don't be rude, introduce yourself to Reverend Rhodes." Mrs. Chastaine gave a nervous smile to the reverend, tapping Oumou gently on the shoulder. "She's a little nervous."

"That is to be expected, given the circumstances," the reverend said, leaning down until he was almost face to face with Oumou. "She's rather outnumbered by people she doesn't know." His breath was hot and smelled sick like melted candy. Her stomach turned at the odor. She dry-heaved as discreetly as possible.

Oumou covered her mouth, hoping to prevent the morning's eggs and sausage from decorating the black stone steps an unseemly new color. "My name's Oumou," she croaked. "Nice to meet you." The last few words trickled off into unintelligible mumbling.

"Well, Oumou," Reverend Rhodes said, straightening back up with all the warmth of a dying mortician. "I'm sure there is a place for you." The statement hung over her head like a pendulous sword.

Oumou opened her mouth to respond, but Mrs. Chastaine ushered her into the sweltering main room of the church. Oumou shuffled past rows of dark wooden pews, worn and weary from near constant use. The pews lined the stone floor that stretched out farther than at first glance. On the back wall, above a simple wooden lectern, a pallid Jesus stared down at the congregation from upon his cross with a pained grimace on his face. The painted blood, drawn from his brow by the meticulously sculpted crown of thorns, ran down his face and spilled onto his shoulders and chest. His body was frozen in the midst of the Passion, contorted so that his muscles strained against the nails through his wrists and ankles. It reminded Oumou of the faces she'd seen at the lab. The other people who'd been there until it was only her left. She couldn't bear to look at it. The sight of the statue mixed with the pulsating heat trapped in the chapel by the heavy stones made her stomach reel. She tugged at Mrs. Chastaine's sleeve to ask where the bathroom was.

"Not right now, Oumou, the sermon is about to begin," came the whisper, harsher than usual. "You need to stay quiet for this."

Oumou curled her knees to her chest and hoped that whatever the sermon was, it wouldn't take too long. She felt the contents of her stomach snaking their way up her throat and didn't know how long she could hold them at bay.

The reverend ascended the steps to the lectern. It looked to Oumou as if each foot placement, each motion his body made, was part of a whole calculated performance. He looked up at Jesus for a long while, hands folded together, before turning to the congregation.

"Hell." The word rolled off his tongue as though he'd said it thousands of times before. "The place of eternal punishment for all sinners."

The tension in the room skyrocketed. Every person stared rapt at the reverend as he spoke. Oumou looked around and realized that she alone had no idea what was going on. Even Amanda watched the man in black with a child-like curiosity. Someone near the front of the church sneezed and was immediately shushed by another attendee.

"There is no want of power in God to cast the wicked into Hell at any moment. He can do so with ease!" He paused, sweeping an arm out over his enraptured audience. "This we are told by the esteemed Reverend Jonathan Edwards, and we see it time and time again in the scriptures. Lot's wife, Sodom and Gomorrah, the unnamed child of David, who paid for the sins of his father, Ananias and Sapphira, who befouled the holy tithe with their lies. God wields the power of condemnation like a mighty sword at all times!"

It was as if everyone in the building was terrified to breath. Even Oumou had to make the conscious effort to exhale a held breath. The reverend commanded attention.

Oumou felt her stomach groan and she retched violently. She hoped no one could hear the gurgling noises it made. A soft breeze of wind slipped through a crack somewhere in the wall and caressed her sweat-dampened skin. The tiny breath of relief wouldn't be enough.

"Vengeance is mine, declares the Lord! But are we not called to do his work? If the Apostles of Christ drove out demons, mustn't we too drive out the demons that invade us? Do we dare stand idly by and let evil and corruption overwhelm us? To bow down to the blackness of sin? Would that not make us wicked, cast rightfully into hell?"

The congregation murmured restlessly. Oumou thought she heard an "amen." A few faces she didn't recognize turned to glare at her, quickly turning their heads when they caught her gaze.

"I come to tell you now that the devil is alive and prowls amongst us even now!" His voice echoed off the black stone walls.

Oumou initially hadn't been paying much attention, but as the reverend spoke, she became painfully aware of a growing tension in the room. His saccharine voice seemed to grate on the panic sensors in her brain.

"We must be suspicious, and skeptical," he continued, "turning away those who would seek to disturb the purity of our town." Oumou could have sworn that he looked directly at her as he spoke the words.

"Well, what about them?" Jim Buckett was standing in front of his pew. The stocky wall of a man was pointing in her direction. "They brought that *girl* into Archwood without even so much as a thought to what she is."

The church fell silent as the weight of the words registered in everyone's mind. Oumou looked to see what the reverend would say, but his thinly veiled smile told her that this was all according to plan. His hands were folded behind his back, and he observed the congregation with an icy gaze.

"Oh, what the hell are you on about, Jim?" Teri heaved herself out of the pew in front of Oumou and placed her hands on her hips. "The girl's more welcome in my store than you are."

The comment got a few laughs from other members of the congregation that cut off quick as Jim glared at the offenders with red-faced fury. "Someone ought to put you in your place, woman," he growled.

"Oh," Vicki Porter rose to her feet, "like how you put poor Leah in her place after you've been drinking. I'll have you know I've reported you to the sheriff the next town over."

"How dare you," Leah said, clutching herself tightly and taking a step away from her husband. "He doesn't...often." She withered under her husband's glare.

"You reported me to Dave?" Jim Buckett said with a laugh. "He's my cousin," he said, "he won't do shit to me."

"Jim," Teri said, "you don't really hit her, do you?"

"This ain't about me," he roared, pointing a furious finger and marching over to jab it into Mr. Chastaine's chest. "It's about these bleeding heart, monkey-loving—"

"Jim," Mr. Chastaine said, his voice completely even, "if you finish that sentence..."

"What?" Jim said with a cruel sneer. "You gonna fight me, doc?" He rolled up his sleeves and put up his fists. "I don't think you got the balls."

"Harold," Mrs. Chastaine whispered, but her husband held up a hand to cut her off.

Mr. Chastaine took a step forward until he was looking down at Jim Buckett. "I know where every bone in your body is located," he said. "I know exactly how much force it would take to break each of those bones, and I know which ones would hurt the most." His face darkened to a frown. "I don't have to fight you," he said. "I just need one good shot."

"You're bluffing," Jim said. He took a hesitant step back.

Mr. Chastaine smiled. "Not to mention that I always carry a few spare scalpels in my coat pocket," he said, reaching inside the suit jacket he wore. "Just in case."

"Beating on you won't even be worth it," Jim said, putting his fists down and returning angrily to his seat in the pew. His wife flinched away as he approached, which only served to worsen his mood. "Damn nigger-lover," he muttered.

Oumou didn't know what that meant, but the entire church erupted into chaos. People rose from the pews shouting and pointing fingers. Mr. and Mrs. Chastaine shifted so that one of them was on either side of Oumou and Amanda. Oumou couldn't fight the urge any longer. Her stomach heaved and she bolted from her seat. Half-digested eggs, bacon, and pancakes forced their way out of Oumou's stomach and splattered on the floor with a wet slopping sound. The Chastaine family looked on in horror, while the people around them scattered to avoid the spray. The conflict in the room froze. Finally, after what felt like hours, Oumou heaved one last time, not able to spit up anything else but bile, and slumped back in the pew. It took her a few seconds to realize that everyone was staring at her.

"Sorry," she croaked. "My stomach—"

A different voice spoke up, a shrill, bird-like squawking. "She can't even stand to be in a house of God!" Sylvia Windsor had risen from her seat, clutching a red leather Bible in shaky hands. "Truly she is the Devil."

"Sylvia," Vicki said with a sigh, "that's ridiculous. This little girl is not the devil. She's just that, a little girl."

"Cast her out!" Sylvia screeched.

"Sylvia," Vicki started.

The reverend watched the proceedings with an icy fascination.

"She befouls our town." Sylvia began to approach the pew where the Chastaines were seated. Her wrinkled face contorted in disgust, deepening the hard lines that criss-crossed her skin. The tension in the room was ramping up again, and Oumou was on the verge of tears. *Why do they hate me?*

"I'm sorry," she whimpered. "I didn't mean to throw up. I can...I can clean it up." She began to lean over, reaching down to scoop the vomit into her hands, but Mr. Chastaine put a firm hand on her shoulder. She looked up at him as tears rolled down her cheeks. He wore a grim expression and shook his head.

"It's okay," he said.

By now the entire church was around them, a mixture of concerned and angry faces looking in on Oumou and the Chastaines. They had no way out.

"Hey, over here." The shutter of a camera clicked at the same time that a flash of light illuminated the darkened interior of the church. In an instant all of the tension and hostility vanished, replaced with confusion. Everyone turned to the back of the church. The sound of a photo being printed from the Polaroid camera chugged along in the now silent chamber. An older black man stood in the open doorway of the church. "Name's Leslie," he said. He flapped the photo back and forth, and blew on it three times, never taking his eyes off the congregation. "Sorry to interrupt, but I just had to snap a picture," he grinned wolfishly. "Awful mighty of you to gang up on a single family like that."

No one said anything.

Leslie looked at the picture. "Oh yeah, that'll look real nice in the paper," he said. "You don't mind, do you?" he asked the reverend.

Reverend Rhodes seethed silently.

"Another one," Sylvia spat. "Like cockroaches."

"And with that, I'm going to scurry on out." He flashed a cheeky smile. "I'm sure I'll see y'all around." He tipped his hat and disappeared back outside the door.

The congregation sat in bewildered silence. No one had the wherewithal to pick up the conflict where it had left off, nor the desire to push forward with any different course of action. They all just stared at the glimmer of sunlight spilling in from the outside.

"What just happened?" the sweaty man from yesterday asked.

The reverend's face twitched with apoplectic rage. "The sermon is over, Donny," he snapped. "Go home, and go with God," he barked, "and be careful where you allot your favor." With an angry flourish, he turned and entered a room at the back of the church, slamming the door behind him. Donny glanced around the room, then scurried after him. Sylvia Windsor followed as well, her nose cast to the sky and a look of holier-than-thou judgment in her beady eyes. No one met her gaze as they parted around to let her pass.

Mrs. Chastaine took Oumou's hand in hers, and together she and the rest of the family walked out of the building, ignoring the remaining stares. She told Oumou to keep her head up. "We will not slink out of this place," she said, a barely controlled fury in her voice. "We will walk proud, hand in hand."

* * *

"Damn that reporter, damn him to Hell!" Reverend Rhodes slammed his fist on his desk, upsetting several books and a pile of papers. He paced back and forth behind his desk. "Things were right where I needed them. I could have driven that girl out with just a word. But now there are two of them crawling around my town." He swiped his arms across the top of his desk, sending everything crashing to the floor. There was a knock at the door.

The reverend slicked back his hair and drew himself up to his full height, putting on a plasticine smile. "Come in," he said, the edge never leaving his voice.

The door creaked open, and Donny Lee peaked his head into the office. "Reverend?"

"Move aside, oaf." Sylvia Windsor shoved Donny into the room, storming in from behind him with her face curled into a furious sneer. "Reverend," she shrieked.

The reverend's eye twitched slightly, but he did his best to remain calm. "Yes, Sylvia?"

"Our town is falling apart before our very eyes," she said. "You must do something."

"I just came to make sure you were okay, rev," Donny said.

"What was that?" the reverend snapped.

"I meant reverend," Donny said. "Sorry, reverend."

"Sylvia," the reverend said, ignoring Donny, "I am well aware of the status of my town. Do you think I am not doing what I must?"

"I think you are," Donny interjected, receiving only a cursory glance from the reverend and a scowl from Sylvia.

"It would seem," Sylvia continued, approaching the reverend and looking up into his cold eyes with her hawk-like stare, "your little show in there didn't work, so I think you know what comes next."

The reverend's eyes narrowed, and his jaw locked tight. His words came out in biting fragments as he spoke. "Do not presume to tell me what to do in my town, woman." The ice behind his eyes sparked into a fiery rage. "Ever."

Sylvia hissed in a breath halfway between fear and anger. She crossed her arms and broke eye contact with the reverend. His fury faded, and his composure returned. He strode to his desk and stooped down to pick the phone up from the floor. He set it gently on the desk, dialed a number, and put the headset to his ear.

"Hello, Leah," he said. "Yes, yes, I know today's sermon was short. Yes, of course. Would you be a dear and put your husband on for me? Busy?" The reverend's tone fell flat. "Please inform him that drinking beer at nine on a Sunday does not constitute 'busy.' Yes, of course tell him that I said it." He drummed his fingers on the top of his desk. "Jim? Gather the boys and keep an eye out for an opportunity to teach that girl a lesson. What? The Chastaines?" He paused for a moment, thinking. "Don't hurt them," he said finally. "I don't care what he said to you," the reverend shouted, "just do as you're told." He slammed the headset into the cradle and took a deep breath, closing his eyes in the process. When he opened them again, they fell on Donny. "Go meet up with Jim Buckett and the others. There is work to do."

"Actually, reverend, uh, I don't really feel comfortable with them," Donny stuttered. "They don't treat me right and—"

By now the reverend had risen from his seat and crossed the room until he stood directly in front of Donny, arms folded across his chest. Donny's words faltered a minute before he continued speaking.

"And besides, she's just a little girl, it don't feel right," he said.

With a quick motion, the reverend backhanded Donny right across his face, knocking the larger man to the ground. "Did that feel right?" he asked.

"No..." Donny rubbed the growing red mark on the side of his face.

"Do you want it to happen again?" The reverend glared down at the man.

"No."

"Then get up off your ass and go find Jim Buckett like I told you to the first time," the reverend hissed.

Donny looked to Sylvia Windsor, who refused to make eye contact with him, instead busying herself with an old portrait hanging on the wall. He looked back to the reverend, who fixed him with an irate stare. "Yes, sir," Donny said, climbing to his feet and exiting the room.

The reverend flicked his eyes over to Sylvia, still staring at the portrait. "What are you still doing here?" he snapped.

"You didn't tell me what to do," she said, regarding him again with her raptor gaze. "So, I'm waiting."

The reverend threw up his hands in frustration. "I don't care what you do," he said. "Go...go separate the troublemaker from the Chastaine girl. You know how Jim gets."

"I say she should be punished too," Sylvia said, "for consorting with—"

"Did I ask?"

Sylvia bit her tongue. "I'll do what I can then," she said.

The reverend raised a hand dismissively, and she exited the room, leaving him at his desk, scrawling away at a new sermon.

* * *

The warm bath soothed Oumou's throbbing head and churning stomach. She sank as low as she could into the soapy water. Slow deep breaths of the steamy air brought her closer to calm. She could hear Mrs. Chastaine's tirade through the thin walls of the house. That was the main thing keeping her from completely relaxing. Another stomp shook the shampoo on the side of the tub.

"Can you believe the reverend just stood there and did nothing?" Elizabeth shouted. "He...he...he should have done something, right?" She paused for an answer.

"Honey, it's not uncommon for certain prejudices to be propagated by religious belief..." Mr. Chastaine said. "He probably wanted that to happen because Oumou's black."

Oumou slid down beneath the water of the tub, anything to drown out the noise. *Black?* she thought. When she couldn't hold her breath anymore, she emerged from the water with a gasp and looked at her arms and legs. *I'm black? And that's why—*

The shouting caught her attention again.

"Why aren't you angry?" she asked, then raising her voice. "Why aren't you angry?"

"I am," he said with a sigh, "but I'm not surprised. I did say it probably wasn't the best idea to take her—"

"Well, I'm sorry for wanting to give a hurting girl a chance to get some of the peace and comfort that I know my God brings to people." It sounded like Mrs. Chastaine was crying now. "Sorry that I expected...that I *hoped* the people who believed in that same God would be better."

Oumou covered her ears and sat in the tub until it sounded like the noises from the next room subsided. She drained the water from the tub, dried off, dressed, and made her way down to the living room.

Mr. and Mrs. Chastaine sat on the suede couch, arms wrapped around each other. Mr. Chastaine stroked his wife's hair as she nuzzled her head into his chest, sound asleep.

"Where's Amanda?" Oumou asked.

"She's sleeping," Mr. Chastaine said, "in her room."

"Oh."

"Oumou..." Mr. Chastaine started.

"Do you hate me because I'm black?" Oumou asked.

Mr. Chastaine's eyes went wide. "You heard?"

Oumou held out her arms in front of her. "I didn't ask to be," she said. "I've been like this since I was born."

Mr. Chastaine kneaded his forehead and dragged a hand down his face. He shifted out from under his wife and put her head on a throw pillow before kneeling down in front of Oumou. "First," he said, "no, we don't hate you over something as silly as the color of your skin. But," he continued, "some people will, because..."

"Because?"

"Because they're afraid," he said.

"Of me?" Oumou asked.

"Hey," Mr. Chastaine said with visible discomfort. He put a hand on her head. "Why don't you go check on Amanda for me, huh?"

"Okay," Oumou said. Before she turned to go to Amanda's room, she added, "I'm glad you're the ones who found me."

She made her way to the other girl's room as quickly as possible. When Oumou arrived, Amanda had moved into the guest room with her and brought some of her toys with her, so Oumou had never actually been inside this room. The walls screamed with a vibrant yellow sheen that hurt her eyes. Stuffed animals lined the twin-sized bed and overflowed beyond its borders, covering the lower portions of all four walls. Amanda lay on the tiny usable portion of the bed, wrapped in white sheets, a purple comforter drawn up over her head. She stirred as Oumou entered.

"Oumou," she said, slurring her friend's name. "Is that you?"

"Yeah. Hi."

"I had a dream about you." She yawned. "It was a good dream." Amanda rolled out of her covers and smiled at Oumou through half open eyes. "You must be tired too." She opened her arms for a hug, toppling plush animals to the floor and making more room on the bed. "There's enough room for both of us."

Oumou smiled and climbed into the bed, tucking herself under the covers next to Amanda. She suddenly felt overwhelmed with her own exhaustion. The two girls fell asleep wrapped in each other's arms.

CHAPTER 8

AMANDA BOUNDED DOWN the stairs with Oumou in tow behind her. "Mom, Dad, can Oumou and I go play out in the vineyard?"

Mrs. Chastaine raised an eyebrow at her husband, who merely shrugged his shoulders. "Sure, I don't see why not, as long as you play safe," he said.

Mrs. Chastaine frowned at him, then rolled her eyes and continued eating. "I guess it's fine then."

"Thank you! Oumou, come on, let's go."

"Whoa there, kiddo. Don't tear her arm off, dragging her like that," Mr. Chastaine said with a laugh. "Be back before it gets dark."

Amanda let go of Oumou's arm and said, "Let's go," before skipping out the door.

Oumou waved an awkward goodbye to the two adults at the kitchen table before following her friend out the door.

* * *

The sun continued its slow ascent into the sky, the early morning light irritating Oumou's eyes still filled with sleep. She rubbed them until they adjusted. She was clothed in one of the outfits Mrs. Chastaine had bought for her. It was far more comfortable than the one from the day before. She and Amanda were wearing the same color, something that made the other girl overtly happy.

The streets were mostly empty; a few people strolled by, most paid no attention to the two little girls. Some stared, or whispered conspiratorially, but no one approached.

Amanda sang a song that Oumou didn't recognize, not that she really knew any songs, but she found herself wondering if the girl simply made up the words as she went along. The little dance that went along with the song was interrupted by the approach of a woman that Oumou recognized from the church. She bored down on them, jaw taut and lips pursed.

"Hi, Ms. Sylvia," Amanda said with a wave. "What are you doing out here?"

"Amanda, why are you still consorting with *her*?" The older woman's grey hair swished furiously behind her, a short cascade of thinning wisps that reached down below her ears.

"She's my friend," Amanda replied cheerily. "I found her in the vineyard two days ago, and my mom, dad, and I are taking care of her."

Sylvia scurried over to Amanda and grabbed her arm with bony fingers, digging into the flesh like crooked claws. "Come away from her at once!"

"No!" Amanda struggled against the older woman's grasp. "Let go! You're hurting me."

"Your parents may choose to do as they wish, but I won't allow you to be tainted by their idiocy," she hissed. "Now, stop this insolence and do as I say."

"But I want to play with Oumou." Amanda flushed as tears streamed down her face. "Mom and Dad said I could."

"That's it," Sylvia said, raising her hand to strike the girl.

"Let her go," Oumou said, wrapping her arms around Amanda and joining in the struggle. She put all her weight into pulling away from the older lady who, despite all appearances, had a nearly superhuman grip on Amanda.

Sylvia rounded on Oumou, her hawk-like eyes glaring. "Let go, mongrel." She gave a forceful tug, and Amanda gasped in pain. Small droplets of blood pooled where her fingernails dug into the girl's soft white flesh.

Seeing the blood sent Oumou into a rage. She flicked her eyes up to Sylvia's face and lashed out, reeling herself in at just the last minute. A force that would have launched her clear across the street became the equivalent of a sharp punch to the face. She didn't want to kill the woman. The last minute focusing of her emotions caused a popping pain somewhere behind her eyes.

Now it was Sylvia's turn to gasp in pain, jerking her hand away from Amanda and touching her nose. Her hand came away bloody. The glare she directed at Oumou quickly became a look of horror. "Monster," she whispered, gathering herself up and storming off in the direction of the church. "You'll get what you deserve," she called over her shoulder.

Amanda rubbed the tiny scratches on her arm, wiping the blood away. Oumou came over and padded the girls arm dry with her shirt. "Are you okay?" she asked.

"She's usually much nicer than that," Amanda said, staring down at the red crescent marks her arm. "Maybe she's had a bad day."

"She doesn't like me," Oumou said.

The girl turned to say something, but stopped, her eyes widening. "What happened to your eyes?"

"What?" Oumou's vision was fine and her eyes didn't hurt. She remembered the pop she'd felt earlier. "What's wrong with them?"

"They're bleeding." Amanda shoved her face as close to Oumou's as possible and reached a hand up towards her face. Oumou pushed it away.

Oumou blinked and what felt like tears dripped from the corners of her eyes. She wiped them away, and blood stained her fingertips. She kept wiping until no more of the substance came away when she touched around her eyes. She looked down at her hands, stained as though she'd broken open a pen on them. Her chest tightened and she felt sick to her stomach.

"I don't—"

"Does it hurt?" Amanda's face clouded with concern.

"No," Oumou said, her voice cracking.

Amanda's face brightened. "Well, Daddy always tells me that if it doesn't hurt, it's probably nothing to worry about."

A wave of relaxation swept over Oumou, until she looked across the street. A man stood against a building back the way they came, watching them. She didn't recognize his face, but she recognized the two eyeless sockets staring out at her. The man's shadow stretched out as though it was reaching for her. She took an instinctive step back. He didn't acknowledge her recognition, just stared, the same inky black substance dripping from the two swirling pits where his eyes were not. The gripping tightness in her chest returned and each breath became more difficult than the last. She turned to Amanda and said, "Let's hurry to the vineyard."

"Are you sure you're okay?" Amanda asked. "We can go get my dad if you want."

"I'm fine," Oumou said, gently tugging the girl in the direction they'd been heading, careful to grab her uninjured arm. "Don't you still wanna go?"

Amanda nodded rapidly with a smile, took Oumou by the hand, and together they set off towards the vineyard.

* * *

"Can we really keep her for this long?" Elizabeth Chastaine asked, her head resting on her husband's lap. He stroked her hair up and down with a purposeful slowness. "I'm getting worried about her staying here, after Sunday."

"I've put out all of my feelers, and no one's reporting a missing black girl," he said. "Either we keep her for now, or we abandon her."

"Harold, she's still a little girl, black or not." She jabbed her elbow into his side as best she could.

"Ouch, I know, I was just being descriptive. Help people know what she looks like and all." He stopped stroking her hair and rubbed his own head. "I know what you mean though...about the locale."

"These aren't *bad* people," she said.

"To us."

Elizabeth sighed. "To us."

"I mean, this isn't exactly the kind of place that historically has been kind to...well, her kind," he said, trying not to sound insensitive.

"But that was years ago. The past is the past. Even here."

"The past is never as far away as we like to think," Harold said.

The sound of glass shattering caused them both to jump. A brick landed on the carpet in front of them. Harold bolted to the window.

"Son of a bitch." Nobody was there, but in their yard stood a cross, burning in the early morning light.

"What is it?" Elizabeth came up behind her husband.

He spun around and ushered her away from the window. "Stay on the couch, I'm gonna use the hose." Harold hurried to the side of the house, turned the water on and dragged the hose, water spraying everywhere, to the front yard. He sprayed the wooden effigy until it was no longer burning. He looked at the charred wooden cross and felt nothing but fury. With a sharp blow from his shoulder, he toppled the structure.

"Oh my God," Elizabeth said, stepping out of the house. "Is that—"

"I told you to stay in the house," Harold shouted.

"Harold," Elizabeth said, "Amanda and Oumou."

"Damn it," he said. "Get in the car."

* * *

The reverend hunched over his large writing desk scowling, already working on next week's sermon to cool his boiling rage. Sleep hadn't stripped it from him, so he'd been up since dawn. He scratched harsh black letters onto the pure white paper, word after word scarring the page. Every sermon he'd ever written had been perfect, save now for one, and he would not let it happen again. A harsh rapping on the rectory door caused his hand to jerk in surprise, tearing a jagged line off the edge of the paper.

"Damn." He crumpled up the paper and tossed into the wastebasket by his side, knocking it over with the force of the throw.

The knocking came again.

"Just come in already," he barked, not even bothering to hide his irritation. He shifted his stack of papers on top of the leather-bound bible on the side of his desk, and steepled his fingers in front him, resting his elbows in the now empty space.

Sylvia stormed into the room, a whirlwind of hair and knobby joints wrapped in perfectly prim clothing. She huffed into the seat across from him, her face red and shining with sweat. Her eyes darted around the room, suspecting everything of conspiring personally against her. The reverend sighed. He didn't have the patience to deal with her two days in a row.

"Good morning—"

"I was assaulted," she screeched, digging her nails into the arms of the chair. "Right here, in our town, reverend! By that little black bitch."

The reverend cleared his throat and attempted to regain control of a situation that already threatened to send him into a fit. "Good morning, Sylvia," he repeated forcefully. "A modicum of decorum, please."

Sylvia looked fit to burst, but she relented. "Good morning, reverend. How are you?" Her grip on the chair did not relax as she spoke.

"I was quite fine, working on a new sermon, you know." His voice fell flat. "Nothing important."

"I—"

"No, no." He waved a hand airily. "It's fine, please, tell me your story. I've already been interrupted." Now that he looked at her, it was quite clear that her nose had been broken. It veered off at a sharp angle that hadn't been there before, and a smattering of dried blood caked her upper lip. The reverend rubbed his temples. "What happened?" He didn't bother trying to sound sympathetic.

"There I was, walking down the street, minding my own—"

"Please, Sylvia, without the theatrics."

"I caught the Chastaine girl walking down the street to the vineyard with the other girl, and I tried to do as you said."

"As I said?" the reverend asked.

"To separate them."

"Ah...yes."

"But then the black girl gets uppity and tries to pull Amanda away from me. So I raise my hand to strike her and—"

"She punched you in the face?"

"No," Sylvia shrieked, "she didn't touch me!"

Edward raised an eyebrow. "She broke your nose...without touching you?"

"Yes, yes, that's what I'm trying to say," Sylvia hissed. "She just looked at me, angry and defiant, and...and then I felt *like* I got punched in the face and my nose was broken."

"She broke your nose...by *glaring* at you?" The reverend barked out a hollow laugh.

"It must be witchcraft," she whispered. "Consorting with the devil's common amongst her kind. That's why it's called black magic."

"Get out."

"I'm sorry?"

"I said, get out of my office before I wring you by your scrawny neck for barging in here with that nonsense."

"Reverend, I'm serious," Sylvia protested.

The reverend watched her face, looking for any sign of deception. Nothing. He took a deep breath, reached across the table and took hold off her nose. With a quick jerk of his wrist, he cracked the nose back into place.

Sylvia gasped in pain and clapped her hands over her nose.

"Better?" the reverend asked.

She nodded and wiped a fresh stream of blood from her upper lip.

He sat back down in his chair and steepled his fingers once more. "Now, Sylvia, I'm sure you just didn't *see* the girl reach out and hit you."

The woman opened her mouth to protest, and he held up a hand to silence her just as the phone rang. He answered. "Yes?"

Sylvia fidgeted uncomfortably in her seat.

"I see," the reverend said. "Yes." He glanced at Sylvia. "Also, it seems that our dear Sylvia has been assaulted." The reverend nodded and rolled his eyes. "Yes, yes you may." He hung up.

"Don't fret, dear woman," he said. "My knights are on their way to bring your assailant to justice."

"Oh, reverend—"

"Now please," the reverend said, crossing the room and holding open the door. "I have somewhere I need to be."

"Where?"

"Away from you," he said, closing the door behind her.

* * *

The grapes were juicy and sweet, and Oumou relished in the fresh natural taste that filled her mouth as she chewed them, one at a time. Amanda sat across from her, her face smeared with grape juice. Oumou watched silently as she ate three, four, and five at a time. The action turned her stomach, but also made her giggle.

"What's funny?" Amanda asked, frowning.

"You are." Oumou's laugh grew louder, stronger. Before she knew it, she was laughing wildly, clutching her sides while the blonde girl looked at her like she grew a second head. It only served to fuel Oumou's laughter.

After a few minutes, Oumou managed to calm herself down, regaining her composure. "Sorry," she said, growing quiet. "You're staring at me."

"I think that's the first time I've heard you laugh," Amanda said.

"Oh..."

"It's a nice laugh."

Oumou felt her face flush with warmth. "You want to see what I can do, right?" she asked. "Like the apples?"

Amanda, who also regained her composure following Oumou's outburst, nodded her head vigorously and jumped to her feet. She opened her mouth wide and pointed to it.

"What are you... Oh, okay." Oumou reached out with her mind, plucked a bunch of grapes off a nearby vine, and moved them to Amanda's mouth. They dangled in front of her. The blonde girl bit down, pulling off three grapes with her teeth. She squealed with delight.

"That's so cool," she said, jumping up and down and clapping her hands.

Oumou, delighted at the prospect that someone genuinely enjoyed what she could do, decided to show off just a little, despite the strain. She lifted some dirt and rocks off the ground. She began to whirl the particles in a circle like the drain in a bathtub, spawning a tiny dust devil in the palm of her hand. Clamping her eyes closed, she lifted the entire phenomena out of her hand and placed it on the ground, sending it up and down the tilled row in which they sat. Her head throbbed, but she pushed through it. The mini tornado accumulated more debris as it went; rocks, grapes, bugs, and twigs, all sucked into the vortex. Enthralled, Amanda chased after it, alternating between trying to catch it and trying to throw things into its cyclonic maw. Oumou couldn't help but smile at the girl's enjoyment.

The smile dropped from Oumou's face when she saw the eyeless man, standing in the next row of the vineyard. He regarded her actions with a cold interest. She kept the cyclone going to distract Amanda and refocused her attention on the figure in front of her. He was different. The first thing Oumou noticed is that he no longer had a burn on his face. The second was that he no longer wore a white coat. His face looked familiar, but she couldn't place why.

"You look different," she said.

"You destroyed my last body," came a deep, sonorous reply. "I took another from the town."

Oumou realized she had seen the man in the church on Sunday. She didn't know his name, but she recognized the face and the build.

"Is he dead?"

"Yes."

Oumou swallowed hard. "Why are you here?"

"I told you already, didn't I? You're mine. I'm going to use your body."

"Like that?"

"Like this."

"So, you weren't just a nightmare," she said. She glanced over at Amanda, who was still chasing the tiny dust devil and tossing grapes and sticks into it, laughing her head off.

The man shook his head slowly. "No."

"I don't want—"

"Oumou, who are you talking to?" Amanda leaned over Oumou's shoulder looking right and left. "There's no one here."

"I, uh, what?" Oumou stuttered.

"Wait," Amanda said, "do you have an imaginary friend too?"

"Yeah, sure," Oumou said, watching the eyeless man with a suspicious gaze.

"Mine is a princess with a sword. She saves animals and beats up mean people. What's your friend like?"

Oumou glanced back at the man in front of her. "He's a guy...with no eyes. And he won't leave me alone."

The figure stared at her silently from behind an unflappable mask of a face. Oumou thought she saw a tinge of anger, but she couldn't be sure. A gust of wind rattled the vines and made the man's hair blow as a cloud of dust passed between them.

"That's weird," Amanda said, sitting down beside Oumou. "I think a sword princess is cooler."

"Yeah," Oumou said. "Much cooler."

The man smirked. "I could claim you right here and now and use your body to tear your little friend apart."

Oumou's eyes narrowed. "I fought you off last time," she said. "If you do whatever you did before, your body will disappear again."

"Last time, I was already weakened. But it is true that you have a strong will, which might be a problem. Luckily there are some people coming who I think will soften you up for me. I'm sure you'll love the fact that they all dress in white." With that, he vanished.

Oumou felt panic rise in her chest. Her pulse quickened. "No," she said.

"Oumou." Amanda cocked her head and put a hand on her friend's shoulder.

Immediately Oumou felt calmer. "We have to go right now," she said. She grabbed Amanda's wrist, careful enough to avoid hurting her, and pulled her in the direction of the town. She skidded to a stop almost as soon as they started running. Between them and the town stood a line of hooded men in white robes. Oumou crouched down to hide just as one of them shouted, "There she is!"

A cold sweat dripped from Oumou's face, and she forced each breath as a painful gasp. *I won't let them take me*, she thought.

"Who are they?" Amanda asked.

Oumou placed a hand over the other girl's mouth and pulled her down to the ground with her. It didn't matter.

"Gotcha," a gruff voice said. Oumou recognized it immediately. It was the short man from the church. Jim, she remembered.

Strong hands yanked Oumou up into the air by the back of her shirt. She started to scream but was interrupted by a heavy punch to the face.

Amanda squeaked with fear.

"Go home, girl," Jim snapped.

"Go," Oumou said as blood dribbled out of her mouth.

"Did I say you could—"

"Hey, she's just doing what you're trying to do," another man said. Oumou didn't recognize his voice.

"Shut up," Jim said. "Get going *now,* girl, this ain't about you."

"But...you're hurting her." Tears filled the corners of Amanda's eyes. She crossed her arms defiantly.

"Your parents spank you, girl?" Jim asked.

"Sometimes," Amanda said, shuffling her feet.

"We're just gonna spank your friend here," he said. "She's been bad."

"My parents are taking care of Oumou," Amanda argued. "If anyone's gonna spank her, it should be them."

"Listen here, you little—"

The second man interjected again. "How about you go get your parents and bring them back here, so we can all talk together? We'll wait for you, okay?"

Amanda thought about this for a minute. Oumou found herself hoping both that she would leave and that she would stay. The pain in her jaw had mounted into a head-pulsing throb, and she felt dangerously close to throwing up.

"Okay," Amanda said, scratching her head. "And Oumou?"

"She has to stay here," said the first man, clearly running out of patience.

Oumou made eye contact with her friend and nodded. "Hurry," she said, forcing a smile.

"Okay." Amanda began sprinting full speed towards town.

"Please hurry," Oumou mumbled as her friend disappeared down the crest of the hill and into the town.

"What was that?" Jim tossed her to the ground.

The smell of dirt and over-ripened grapes filled her nose and mouth. Oumou felt a tooth chip on a rock, tearing a hole in her lip as she hit the ground. She immediately began to try and crawl away, but the hooded men quickly surrounded her.

"Let me go," Oumou said through gritted teeth.

"Oh, we'll let you go, after we finish our *talk,*" Jim said, crouching down over her. "At least that's what we told your little friend..."

Oumou tried to get to her feet, but he stomped his boot down into her back. She felt the air leave her lungs. He used the toe of his boot to roll her onto her back before pressing his foot down right in the center of her chest. His weight prevented her from moving at all.

The man leaned down until his face was only inches away from hers. "You got no right to be in our town, girl."

"Get. Off. Of. Me." Oumou groaned. She slammed her fists into his leg as hard as she could. Her hands scrambled around at her side until they found a rock. She jammed it into the side of Jim's leg.

"Damn it," he shouted, jerking his leg into the air and then slamming it back down into her chest. "I'll kill you, little bitch," he said, forcing more of his weight onto her. Some of the other men tried to pull him off her.

"This wasn't the plan."

"Stop it, that's enough."

The voices around her began to all blend together. Jim shook the other men off him and continued pressing down on Oumou's chest. She tried to breath, but the air lodged itself in her chest like a dagger. Her lungs burned, and her head throbbed. Panic coiled around her heart like thorny vines. The world around her began to darken. She couldn't think. All of the strength left her arms and she was no longer able to struggle against the weight of his boot on her chest. She looked up at the hooded man looming over her. Her head swam, but beneath the panic and the darkness threatening to swallow her up she felt something else, something white-hot and burning at the very core of her being. She felt rage, and she reached for it, pulling it to the surface and letting it loose just as everything went dark.

Oumou rose from the ground, facing down the gathered robes who watched in disbelief as she floated above them. Her eyes had rolled back into her head and she spoke in a shrill screech. "Never again," she roared. A wave of force rushed out from her, toppling the robed men. The rows of vines around them shuddered violently as she hung above them like a wrathful angel. All manner of debris swirled in the air around them, nicking and tearing the men's robes, leaving tiny stains of blood where they struck.

The men scrambled to their feet and ran. Jim tried to follow them, but his body went rigid, frozen to the spot. He spun around to face Oumou, her face hidden behind a wall of dust. A sound like lightning striking a tree echoed through the vineyard and Jim screamed as his femur broke, snapping sideways and jutting out at a wrong angle. Another crack, and another scream. The man's bones twisted, creaking and snapping as they did, until every single one was completely deformed. There was one last gunshot report and his body crumpled in on itself like a balled-up wad of paper and dropped to the ground. Oumou's empty eyes regarded the body before turning to watch the other men, still fleeing back towards the town. She felt the rage inside begin to subside, and as it did she snapped back to consciousness and dropped from the sky. She let out a pained gasp as she slammed into the dirt.

Her whole body throbbed, and each breath felt like a knife to her lungs. She struggled to her feet and swayed uneasily as lightheadedness swept over her. The dead man's body lay crumpled in front of her, a pool of blood soaking into the dirt around it. His hood had come off. Jim's glassy, red-rimmed eyes stared up at her from overtop a mouth contorted with fear and lifeless hatred.

Oumou tried to scream but no sound came out. The act only hurt her chest. Her stomach turned and she tried to hold in a surge of vomit. The acrid taste filled her mouth and she spat it onto the ground. Another pain spiked in her chest as she heaved. She looked away from the staring eyes and moved to another row of the vineyard.

The pain made it hard for her to focus. She shuddered, despite the warmth of the afternoon sun. *Mr. Chastaine could help,* she thought. *He's a doctor.* Oumou slowed her breathing. It still hurt, but she was able to gulp down the oxygen which helped to settle her lightheadedness. She took a single laborious step towards the town. *I have to get back.* She took another step. *Amanda is probably worried.*

With that thought, she began a slow trudge back towards the town.

* * *

Leslie watched the girl limp back towards the town. He stared down at his camera, his mind replaying everything he just saw in slow motion. *That power,* he thought. The Klansmen hadn't stood a chance. *Serves them right, ganging up on a little girl like a bunch of cowards.* He felt a pang of guilt in his chest. *Not that you're much better.* Leslie had seen the men approaching long before the girl did.

"And what'd you do?" he asked no one in particular. "Not a damn thing."

Magnum barked.

"Yeah, guess she didn't need our help after all, but still," he said. "Should we go check it out?"

Another bark.

"Yeah, let's go."

He snuck over to the aftermath, stopping every so often to make sure no one else was entering the vineyard. Along the way he tripped and fell into a crater that he hadn't seen from up by the woods.

"The fuck?" he said, snapping a picture once he'd crawled out of the indentation in the ground.

Finally he got to the place where the attempted lynching took place. He looked down at the corpse of the Klansmen with a hand pressed over his mouth. If Leslie hadn't seen what the man looked like before, he wouldn't have been able to tell the twisted mound of flesh had once been a man. Leslie winced as he remembered the gunshot sounds as his bones broke, one at a time and then suddenly all at once.

He shuddered and turned to Magnum. "You much of a digger?"

Magnum laid down under a tangle of vines and panted at him lazily.

"Figures."

Leslie knelt down and scraped his hands through the soft and loamy dirt. Digging through it would be easy, but he still wished he had a shovel. He dug until he had a hole deep and wide enough to fit the body. He looked up in the sky at the sun now hanging halfway between noon and sunset. The burnt skin on his neck and arms stung as a cool breeze caressed his skin. He stood up and walked around the other side of the body. One forceful shove with his foot sent the bag of bones tumbling into the pit. He scuffed his boot in the dirt to rub off any blood that may have clung to it.

"What purpose did that serve?"

Leslie jumped back from the pit and clutched at his camera. The King of Thorns towered over him in a new body, his dark eye sockets impossibly black in the bright sun. Magnum barked in surprise at the thing's sudden appearance.

"I couldn't just leave him here." Leslie threw the first handful of dirt on the body.

The King of Thorns' face contorted into a sneer. "You hate this man."

Leslie noticed that the flesh around the body's neck was already beginning to burn away. The King of Thorns adjusted the collar of his shirt.

"You're right," Leslie said. "I hate him. I hate what he stands for, I hate what he did to that girl, and I hate that there are others like him. Yeah, I hate him."

"Yet you honor him with a grave?"

Leslie spat on the body in the pit and kicked in another pile of dirt. "It ain't for him. It's for...the girl." *The girl you just saw turn a man into a Gordian knot.* "I leave the body out, it's evidence they can use against her."

"Remember my warning."

Leslie glared up at the demon, guilt fueling his anger. "You know what I'd like more than anything in the world right now?"

The King of Thorns raised a disinterested eyebrow.

"For you to fuck off right now." He tossed a handful of dirt at his face and regretted it immediately. *I'm going to die,* he thought.

There was a moment of tense silence. Leslie felt his heart pounding in his chest as two eyeless voids stared down at him. His knees began to wobble as the moment stretched on forever. Leslie thought he'd go mad as the sweat dripped icily down his back, causing him to shudder despite the evening heat.

The King of Thorns grunted in disapproval and vanished, melting away into its own shadow. Leslie collapsed to his knees, gasping. He waited for a searing pain, or the ice-cold grip of a thousand dead hands, or just instant death, but nothing came. He sighed and stared down at his trembling hands clutching handfuls of dirt. Magnum trotted over and licked at his knuckles.

"Yeah," Leslie said, "we got a job to finish."

The dead man stared up at him from the shallow grave as Leslie shoveled handful after handful of dirt onto his body. Magnum also began kicking dirt back into the hole as well. When he finally finished, for the second time in the past few days, Leslie prayed.

"Don't let me end up like him," he said, wiping the dirt from his hands. "I ain't done nothing half as bad, so cut me some slack."

"Glad you wouldn't listen when I told you to stay in the house?" Leslie asked Magnum, wiping sweat from his brow. "Hell of a show, huh?"

The dog bumped against his arm and panted happily.

"Yes, that's the one you fucked up with those teeth of yours, and *yes,* it hurts." He reached out his other arm to pat the dog on the head. "Motherfucker," he said with a smile.

Magnum barked, his tail wagging like an out-of-control metronome.

"I don't speak dog." Leslie thought for a moment. "You're hungry, aren't you?"

Magnum barked again.

"Okay, okay, must you be so loud?"

The dog's third bark clearly meant "yes."

Leslie turned towards the town and sighed. "Racists, magic girls, shadow demons, and a dog that's always hungry. I should have stayed my ass in New York."

Leslie patted down his jacket and found the lump in his pocket. He pulled the flask out and took a long swig, draining all but the last sip of the burning liquid. He shook his head. "Son of a bitch... You saw that too, right?" He turned so he was cross-legged, facing the dog.

Magnum just stared at him.

"They were all around her and then...*boom,* she goes all wrath of God on their asses." He rubbed the back of his neck. "Good thing we didn't get involved... That could have been us. Right, boy?"

The fur on Magnum's neck began to stick up, and a low rumble began to rise from his throat. He began to back away from Leslie and the grave.

"Magnum?"

The rumble in Magnum's chest morphed into a fit of angry barking at something behind Leslie. The hairs on the back of Leslie's neck stood on end. He swallowed hard. Despite everything in his being telling him not to look, Leslie turned to look behind him. The corpse was standing in his grave. His limbs cracked and dangled, blood and black fluid dripped down his body. A low, rasping moan escaped from his throat as he took a single janky step towards Leslie, arms outstretched and hands grasping.

Leslie scrambled to his feet. "No!" He couldn't form any other words, just repeated the same word over and over again. He tried to run, but fear froze him to the spot.

The dead man reached out to Leslie and dragged a single bloody hand down his face. A bloody grin stretched stiffly across the corpse's sunken face. He opened his mouth wide until the skin at the corners of his mouth began to tear, dripping coagulated blood to the ground in little clumps.

Two words gurgled out from the back of his throat, making Leslie gag. "Fuck...off."

With a lumbering step, the corpse turned and shambled back to the makeshift grave, clawing his way beneath the earth and finally disappearing beneath the loamy vineyard soil.

Leslie stood still bolted to the spot for a moment, until a bark from Magnum snapped him back to reality. He shakily reached for his flask but stopped when he remembered that it was empty.

"Let's get out of here," he said.

When they got back to the cabin, the first thing Leslie did was raid the cellar for another bottle of whiskey, taking a long drink and settling on the floor against a wall. The shaking in his hands began to still, and he finally felt calm enough to think through his situation. *So that's the girl.*

"She's not gonna be safe down there," he said, rubbing Magnum on the head. "Not anymore." He sighed. "Guess we're making one hell of an enemy starting today, huh?" He took another pull from the bottle. "I'm nobody's damn slave."

CHAPTER 9

THE CHASTAINES' CAR pulled up alongside Oumou about halfway between the vineyard and their home. Mrs. Chastaine leapt from the car before Mr. Chastaine could properly stop the vehicle.

"Oumou," she shouted, pulling the girl into a tight embrace.

Oumou gasped in pain, and Mrs. Chastaine released her, stepping back and holding Oumou at arm's length. When she saw Oumou's state, she gasped, and tears began to form at the corners of her eyes.

"Harold," she called.

Her husband put the car in park and jogged over to them. "Oh my god," he said. "I'll be right back." He was back in a few seconds with his medical bag. Oumou jumped as the cold metal of a stethoscope pressed against her chest. "Breathe," Mr. Chastaine said. He listened to her lungs for a few seconds before saying, "Nothing's punctured her lungs, at least." His fingers pressed around her ribs and chest. Oumou let out a pained gasp. "There may be some fractures, but nothing feels broken or out of place." He stood up and gave Oumou a sympathetic look. "But it definitely hurts, doesn't it?"

Oumou nodded slowly. "Yes."

"What happened?" Mrs. Chastaine asked.

"Is Amanda okay?"

"She's fine, in the back seat of the car. Oumou, what happened?"

"Men in white robes hurt me," Oumou said.

"How did you get away?"

Oumou remembered the dead man in the vineyard and the fear on the faces of the other men as they ran away. "They...I...uh, I ran," she said finally. "When they weren't looking."

"Are they still up there?" Mr. Chastaine asked.

"I don't think so," Oumou said.

"Bastards," he spat.

"They said I needed to be punished." She looked at Mr. Chastaine. "Is it because...?"

Mr. Chastaine nodded, a solemn look on his face.

"I should leave," Oumou said. The shock that the bluntness of her statement caused was clear on both of the adults' faces. "I'm not welcome."

"Oumou," Mrs. Chastaine said with a sad smile. "No." She wrapped gentle arms around the girl. "I'm so sorry about this."

Mr. Chastaine pushed his hands deep into the pockets of his jeans. "It's safer for you to stick with us. We should have kept a better eye on you," he said.

"But they'll hurt me again... They'll hurt Amanda," Oumou said. "And you."

"No, no," Mrs. Chastaine said. "We'll be fine."

"Amanda would want you to stay," Mr. Chastaine said. "We'll take care of you. Promise."

"Like our own daughter," Mrs. Chastaine added.

A tear ran down Oumou's face. Another followed suit. Then another. Before she knew it, she was sobbing, pressing her face against Mrs. Chastaine's soft sweater. Oumou couldn't remember the last time she'd really cried. It wasn't a cry of panic or fear, but a truly cathartic release of years of pent-up emotion. She cried while Mrs. Chastaine led her to the car and opened the door to the back seat.

Oumou got in and was immediately confronted by Amanda's concerned face.

"You're okay," the girl said, bouncing in her seat. "I was so worried, I ran all the way until Mom and Dad found me. I made them hurry back and now we found you."

She pulled Oumou in for a side hug. Oumou smiled at the warmth. "I'm okay," she said. "Thank you."

Whatever adrenaline had kept Oumou going began to wear off, and her whole body, still throbbing, began to feel heavier until she could barely keep her head upright. Her head lolled to the side, resting on Amanda's shoulder.

"It's okay," Amanda said, "you can rest now. You look tired."

* * *

The reverend paced around the office, wondering how Jim and the others were doing with their task. His answer came in the form of Donny's barging into the office unannounced. The man dripped with sweat and his chest heaved from the exertion of running all the way from the vineyard. He looked longingly at the chair across from the reverend's desk. The reverend did not ask him to sit.

"Donny."

"His bones. Twisted. Broken. Dead." The man broke down. "She...she killed him, reverend."

"Donny." The reverend rose from his seat and slammed his fist onto the desk. "Quit blubbering and speak clearly."

Donny flinched away. "Okay," he said. "Okay." He began breathing deeply to try and steady himself. "The girl, reverend, she killed Jim."

The reverend leaned forward, a frown darkening his face. "How?"

The other man's eyes widened, and he looked close to spiraling into a full-on panic again. "I don't know," he whispered. "One second he was fine, and then...dead."

"My patience for you is growing thin," the reverend growled. His fists clenched into white-knuckled balls of anger. "You barge in here unannounced with a story about a girl no older than twelve *killing* Jim Buckett, and you can't even tell me how it supposedly happened?"

"I don't—"

"Know? So you've said."

"She was flying, and...and her eyes were all white—"

One of the reverend's many paperweights exploded against the wall behind Donny. The reverend stood, hand outstretched, face contorted with fury. "Enough of your nonsense," he said. "She is a *child*. She is *nothing*."

"But, reverend," Donny said, "I'm not lying."

The reverend thought about Sylvia's story from earlier, and now Donny's. He sat back in his chair with a sigh and fixed the loose strands of dark hair hanging in front of his face. *Black magic*, he thought. His eyes locked onto Donny's. "Tell me everything that happened in as much detail as possible," he said.

When the man finished his story, the reverend had to clench his jaw to keep a straight face. Donny fidgeted nervously where he stood, glancing around as if he were afraid the girl might crawl out from the walls and attack him.

The reverend rubbed the stubble on his chin and gazed thoughtfully at the wall. "Where is Jim's body?"

"Still out in the field, I guess," Donny said. His eyes widened. "Please don't make me go back out there, reverend. I can't, I'm too scared." He wrung his hands nervously, cracking and popping joints in the process.

"I wouldn't send *you* back out," the reverend said. "Where are the others?"

Donny gulped. "They all quit," he said. "Threw out their robes and went back home."

"Cowards."

"Don't blame them, reverend. I could barely believe what I saw," Donny said. "I thought for sure I was dead. Never ran so fast in my life. And I came right here to tell you."

"Small victories," the reverend muttered. His gaze snapped back to Donny as he forced down the combination of fear and rage that boiled up inside of him. "You know what this means," he said.

"What?"

"I was right." A gleeful grin steeped in malice spread across the reverend's face. "My sermon," he said. "The devil walks among us."

"Is that...good?" Donny asked.

"What?"

"You just seem happy about it," Donny said. "But it sounds bad."

"I'm happy" — the reverend sneered — "because I can use this against her. I can use Jim's death to turn the whole town against her. They'll tear her apart."

Donny blanched. "But Jim—"

"Jim is dead," the reverend snapped. "And besides, he'd want this, don't you think?"

"I guess..."

"You guess?"

"Well, I mean, why don't we just leave her alone?" Donny asked.

"Excuse me?" The reverend's icy demeanor returned.

"I just, you know, after the church, and now this, she probably won't want to stay for too much longer, right?" Donny waited for the reverend to respond and, receiving nothing, continued. "Why don't we just wait her out?"

"And let her get away with what she did to Jim? After the way she and that reporter embarrassed me in front of my congregation?" The reverend's eyes narrowed, and he regarded Donny as one might a worm or other small insect.

"But if we wait for her to leave, you can still say that it was you who got rid of her," Donny said. "No one would know."

"I don't want her gone," the reverend roared, striking Donny across the face with his open hand. "I want her dead!"

Donny raised his arms in front of his face, cowering behind them as he spoke. "I'm sorry, I just thought—"

"Well, don't," the reverend spat. "It doesn't suit you." He loomed over Donny, hand still raised as if to strike him again. There was a glint in his eyes as he spoke again. "You know, Donny," he said. "You're pitiful."

"I...I am?"

"People didn't like Jim, they knew what an ass he was, but you...people feel bad for you. They would...sympathize with you." He lowered his hand and circled around to the other side of his desk, picking up another paperweight, one shaped like a mountain, and bouncing it in his hand. He circled back around and stood in front of Donny with an inscrutable look on his face.

"Reverend, I don't understand," Donny said.

"You think we should just let that uppity little brat parade around our town as she pleases?"

"She was just playing when we got there," Donny said. "She wasn't doing any harm. We attacked her first."

The reverend's face twitched. "First?" His voice rose in volume until he was shouting again. "She attacked us the moment she set foot in this town. Her presence alone is a declaration of war against our pure and perfect community."

"I don't think—"

The reverend slammed the mountain-shaped paperweight into the side of Donny's head with a sickening crunch. Donny staggered backwards, slamming into the door behind him. He felt around for the doorknob but found that it had been locked. Blood trickled down his face, turning his vision a blurry red.

"Reverend, please," he said.

"You think I should just stand around while that mongrel spreads its filth around *my* town?" The reverend stalked up to him, paperweight still slick with blood held firmly in his hand. "That I should lay myself low and submit to *her* whim?" The reverend brought his knee up between Donny's legs as hard as he could and watched with satisfaction as the man dropped to the ground. The reverend's breathing was heavy from the exertion and the exhilaration. He dropped the paperweight to the floor.

"I'm sorry," Donny whimpered.

"Not yet," the reverend said.

The first punch didn't give the satisfying crunch that the reverend wanted, so the second time he aimed for Donny's nose. The cartilage crunched beneath his fist, and a warm spray of blood slickened the reverend's knuckles. His own ragged breathing sent a shudder of pleasure down his spine. He punched the man again and again until he could no longer raise his fist without being overwhelmed by exhaustion.

"Letting them do what they want is what got my father killed," the reverend hissed. "I'll not make the same foolish mistake."

Donny didn't say anything. His upper body was slumped slightly over his knees and his breathing came in quick, shallow bursts.

"Answer me, damn you." The reverend's voice was little more than a hoarse scream.

Donny looked up, his swollen face smeared with blood, unfocused eyes searching until they landed on him. The reverend saw something there that he'd never seen in the man's eyes before. He saw defiance.

Donny spat a slow dribble of blood and saliva to the floor. "I looked up to you," he said, lurching over with a violent cough as he did. "Thought you were in complete control." He looked back up at the reverend, his eyes crystal clear. "But one little black girl stumbles into your town and you lose control." He coughed out a chuckle. "You're as pathetic as I am," he said.

The reverend let loose a furious scream and lunged at the man, wrapping his hands tight around his thick throat and squeezing with all his might. He jammed his thumbs into the man's airway and pressed his head into the floor with all his might. Donny sputtered and choked but didn't take his eyes off the reverend until they rolled back in his skull and his body went limp. A single last rattling gasp escaped from his throat as the reverend released his grip. He hovered over the body, taking in each breath as though it would be his last.

"Damn you, Donny Lee," he gasped. "At least now you'll be useful."

The reverend froze as someone knocked on the door. He searched the office for a place to hide the body but realized he couldn't easily move the man lying on the floor. The knock came again.

"Reverend?" Sylvia called. "Are you in there?"

The reverend cracked open the door, keeping the body and his bloody clothes out of view. Sylvia stared back at him suspiciously.

"What do you want?" he asked.

The woman leaned around to look past him into the office. With a hiss, the reverend grabbed her by the wrist and jerked her into the room, locking the door behind her. Sylvia gasped when she saw the body lying on the floor.

"What have you done?" she asked.

"Not me," the reverend said shakily. "The girl."

"What?"

"I said the girl killed him," he said, rounding on her. There were tears in his eyes. "You were right about the black magic."

"I don't understand," Sylvia said, pressing her back up against the locked door.

"Donny came in here in a panic," he said, spinning his web. "He said the girl had killed Jim when they went after her. That she used some kind of dark powers. And as he stood there before me, his head began to bleed as though he'd been struck." He paused to gauge Sylvia's reaction before continuing. "I went to help him" — he gestured at his bloodstained clothes — "but it was too late. Whatever she'd done to him...well, you can see for yourself." He sunk down into his chair and held his head in his hands.

"Reverend, are you sure?" Sylvia asked.

"What else could it be?" he moaned. He looked up at the sound of something thudding on his desk.

Sylvia placed a revolver on his desk and slid it towards him. "For protection."

The reverend blinked rapidly in confusion. "Where did you even get that?"

"It was my late husband's," she said. "I kept it after he died."

"Why give it to me?"

"She might come after you," she said. "Now, go wash up."

"Yes, but...what about the...what about Donny?" The reverend put on his most sympathetic face. "We can't just leave him here like this."

"Do you serve the Lord?" Sylvia held his gaze with a manic passion.

"I do," the reverend said.

"Then I serve you," she said. "Go; I'll clean up the mess and we can handle the body together."

"Are you sure?" the reverend said. "I feel like I should do something. To inconvenience you so much—"

"Go."

The reverend made his way to the door and unlocked it. As he exited the room, a wide smile cracked his face. "Thank you so much, Sylvia," he said. "This means so much to me." The door creaked shut behind him and he made his way to the shower at the back of the church.

CHAPTER 10

A KNOCK ON the door in the middle of the night was never a good thing in Leslie's experience. Even less so when no one was supposed to know where you were. He took a moment to be thankful that Magnum hadn't immediately started barking at the sound. The knock came again. Leslie crossed the wooden floor as quietly as he could, taking care to avoid the panels that he knew squeaked. There was no peephole on the door like at his apartment, so he shifted the curtains of the nearest window ever so slightly. He hoped the darkness of the night would cloak his investigation.

A single police officer stood on the cabin's dilapidated front porch. He shined the light of his flashlight towards the window just as Leslie ducked back behind the curtain, holding it in place so the movement wouldn't give him away.

"Look, I know someone's in there," the officer called out. "Got a fresh set of tracks leading right up to the front door."

"Fuck," Leslie whispered. He tried to stay as still as possible, hoping that a lack of response would make the man give up.

"Since no one owns this place," the officer continued, "I do not need a warrant to enter. I'm giving you a chance to let me in of your own accord. You have until five before I kick in the door."

Leslie hesitated.

"Five," the man said. "Four...Three...Two—"

"I wouldn't do that," Leslie called out. "The dog won't like it too much."

"Then are you going to let me in?"

"Leave your gun on the porch," Leslie said. "I'm unarmed and I'd feel much more comfortable if you were as well."

"How's that?"

"My skin seems to attract more bullets than it's worth," Leslie said.

Silence from outside. "I understand. I am holding up my gun and putting it on the ground."

Leslie peaked through the window and saw that the man had in fact complied, placing the heavy Colt on the porch. The officer put his hands on his head and stared expectantly at the window. Leslie made his way to the door, unlocked it, and slowly peered around as he opened it. The cop's pearly white teeth smiled wryly at him from a dark and weathered face. "What was all that about attracting bullets?" he asked.

"Don't think I like you any more just 'cause you look like me, cop," Leslie said. "Get in and leave the gun out there."

"I just came to talk," the cop said, stepping into the cabin.

"I know how your kind 'talk,'" Leslie said. "Sit down." He pulled out a chair on one side of the dust-covered kitchen table and slid himself into the opposite seat. His back was to the busted window, an escape route if needed. The cop seemed to notice as well, his eyes flicking momentarily to the window before settling back on Leslie.

"So..." the cop said.

"So?"

"You want to tell me what you're doing out here all by your lonesome?"

"I'm not alone," Leslie said, gesturing at Magnum. "I got myself a dog."

"That wasn't my question, son." The chair squeaked as the cop leaned back in his seat, folding his hands across his chest.

"I'm not your son," Leslie said. He drummed his fingers on the table. "Get to the point and tell me why you're here."

"What do you know about the bar on the south end of the woods?" the cop asked.

"Not a goddamn thing," Leslie said.

"Nothing at all?" The cop raised an eyebrow.

"It's a shitty dive bar," Leslie said with a shrug, "and they don't take too kindly to folks like...me."

"Like us," the cop said.

"Sure."

"So, you admit you've been there at least once?" the cop continued, ignoring Leslie's jab.

"Found myself hauling ass, hoping they didn't catch up to me," Leslie said. "Didn't exactly make me want to go back for a second visit."

The cop nodded his head slowly, looking around the room as he did. "Name's Carver," he said. "Carver McKay."

"Don't recall asking," Leslie said. "Can't say I care."

"Look, man, it's just us here, we don't have to be enemies," Carver said.

"We became enemies the moment you put on that badge."

"All right," Carver sighed. "Business only. Where were you three nights ago?"

"My apartment in New York."

"Why are you here?"

"I'm a reporter. Got a tip there might be a story down here," Leslie said, pointing to his camera resting on a nearby countertop.

"A story in North Carolina for a New York newspaper?"

"We're trying to diversify our stories," Leslie said with a shallow smile. "Why are you here, exactly?"

The cop leaned forward, placing his hands flat on the table. "People died in that bar down on the south side of the forest. A lot of them. In a bad way."

"And you think...I had something to do with it?"

"I think I just learned there's a strange new man living in an abandoned cabin in the woods a few days after an unholy massacre took place," Carver said. "That's what we cops call 'suspicious'."

Leslie rocked back farther in his chair until he was balancing on the back two legs. "So, a bunch of racists die in a backwater bar and they send out your black ass to investigate?"

Carver shook his head. "I came out here on my own," he said. "Department already found a culprit. Young kid." He paused. "Black."

Leslie winced. He tried to play it off. "Then why come out here bothering me if they found their guy?"

"I said *a* culprit, not *the* culprit," Carver said. "Something about it didn't sit right with me. The evidence was all—"

"Fake," Leslie finished.

"Too convenient," Carver said. "Dave, the sheriff, had mentioned losing a dog out here" — he looked at Magnum — "when they were chasing the suspect. So, I figured here was as good a place to start."

"How'd you know I was in here?" Leslie asked.

"I didn't until you answered," Carver said with a smile.

"Son of a" — Leslie dragged his hands down his face — "bitch," he finished.

"I get that you don't trust me," Carver said, "and it's a good reason. But I'm trying to change the shit from the inside. I can't let them kill this boy if he ain't the one. So please, tell me what you know."

Leslie fixed the cop with a bitter stare. He drummed on the table until he felt like his fingers might snap off and crawl away. Carver held his gaze.

"First, I didn't do it," Leslie said. "You want anything out of me, you've gotta start by believing that."

"I can do that."

"Second, you aren't gonna believe a word out of my mouth, but it's God's honest truth."

Carver again raised a single eyebrow. "All right, shoot," he said.

When Leslie finished his story, he shifted awkwardly in his chair and watched the cop's face for any indication of what his reaction would be.

Carver's face showed a mixture of disbelief and concern. He sighed and put down his pen and notepad. "I thought you said you were gonna level with me."

"I know how it sounds," Leslie said. "But it's all true."

"You expect me to believe something out of a pulp novel?" He paused and scratched his head. "Way I see it," Carver said, "the only believable parts of that tale are that you were at the bar the night of the massacre, and that there may be a young negro girl stuck up in Archwood."

"So, is this the part where you arrest me then?" Leslie said, sticking his wrists out across the table. "Drag me in and swap me out for the boy you got in your cells back home?"

Carver gave him a wry smile. "No, sir," he said. "I got no evidence. Nothing to link you to the murders. Sure, you told me you were there and went off on some fancy-ass story, but for all I know, you could've just escaped while the killer was preoccupied."

Leslie retracted his arms and folded them across his lap. "You're for real?"

"Besides, I think if you were the killer, you'd have had a better story than that. A man with no eyes? Flying girls?" He nodded his head as if he were certain. "Shock's what it is."

"Yeah," Leslie said. "Shock."

"Now, about that girl up in Archwood. She yours?" Carver asked.

"Absolutely not," Leslie said.

"You know her folks?"

"No."

"That's no good," Carver said. "That's no good at all."

"No good?"

"Well, you said yourself that they tried to lynch her and she got away, but I'm sure they'll try again." Carver rubbed the greying beard on his chin.

I wouldn't be so sure, Leslie thought. "They won't just give it up?" he asked.

"There have been quite a few lynching's up there since the new reverend took over the place. None recently, but within the past ten years...lots," Carver said. "I've taken to warning folks about even passing through the town, let alone being there after sundown."

"So, she's still in danger," Leslie said. *Of course she is. More than you know.* "Why don't you go get her out of there?"

"No jurisdiction," he said. "And besides, just because I wear this badge...don't mean they're gonna respect me any more than they do you. That glint of gold is never gonna draw their eye away from the color of my face." He rose from his seat and extended a hand to Leslie. "I thank you for your cooperation."

Leslie stared at the man's hand, sucked his teeth, and gave one quick, firm shake before crossing his arms once more. "You can see yourself out."

"You're right about that," Carver said. He stopped at the door. "A word of advice," he said. "Brother to brother. Get out before this place kills you." The cop stopped at the porch and replaced his gun in its holster.

"Hey," Leslie called.

Carver turned. "Something else?"

"Let me know what happens," Leslie said. "With the kid."

"And if it's bad news?"

"It will be." Leslie held up a half-empty bottle of whiskey. "But we'll share a drink in his honor."

"Thought you hated cops?"

"I do, but I recognize that a brother may need someone to drink with when shit gets dark." Leslie didn't cheapen his statement with a smile.

"That might be nice," Carver said as he descended the creaking steps. He stepped onto the grass and paused a moment, looking up at the stars before setting off and disappearing into the woods.

"So that's why I didn't see him coming," Leslie mumbled. "He literally came out from the woods." He turned to Magnum. "Thanks for putting that dog nose to good use," he quipped.

Magnum yawned.

When the officer was out of sight, Leslie began to search the house for anything that might help him with his plan. He pulled open a drawer in the kitchen and saw the silver glint of a handgun. The size and weight felt perfect. He checked the clip.

"Only three?" He scrounged around in the drawer, his hand finding only crumpled papers before he felt a few more stray bullets. He reached all the way to the back, and something crawled away just as his fingers brushed it. "And we're done," Leslie said, pulling his hand from the drawer. "Just have to make these count then."

He pulled on his trenchcoat and stuffed the gun in the side of his waistband after ensuring the safety was on. His hat he pulled down low, hoping to obscure his face until the absolute last possible minute. He checked his watch. 8:00pm. It was probably an hour walk to the town. *Hope I don't miss all the action*, he thought wryly.

"You coming, Magnum?" he asked. "Tonight we enter the line of fire."

Magnum's yawn and the subsequent adjustment to his sleeping position said, "No, tonight *you* enter the line of fire."

"Lazy bastard," Leslie said. "Fine. Sleep well. Got a feeling you're going to need it."

CHAPTER 11

OUMOU'S SLEEP THAT night teemed with nightmares. In her dream, the men that experimented on her wore white robes with pointed hoods in place of labcoats. They stared down on her with the lifeless black voids that shadowed their eyes. She looked around and found that she was strapped on a steel table, her arms and legs held in place by thick leather straps.

"You killed him," they chanted as they wheeled her down a seemingly endless hallway, past open doors from which the eyeless man watched her, growing closer as they passed each open portal.

"I didn't mean to," she shouted back. "He was hurting me."

They ignored her cries, still chanting their monotonous judgment. She tried to fight her way out of the restraints, but the more she struggled, the tighter the leather seemed to squeeze around her wrists and ankles. They slammed her head back down as she tried to lift it up and look around. It hit the cold metal gurney. Hard. She could feel the icy cold of the metal skittering across her skin. All she could do was stare up at the ceiling as they carted her to her destination. A feeling of dread began to fester in the pit of her stomach. The hallway was beginning to look familiar, and she knew where they were taking her. Oumou began to scream and struggle with all her might, but to no avail. She tried to free herself with her mind, but only received a ringing in her ears for her efforts.

"Please," she cried. "No!"

The gurney stopped suddenly, jerking Oumou's head forward and then slamming it back against the cold surface. The chanting stopped, and the robed men broke their circle to make way for a new figure.

"It seems the experiment was a failure," the eyeless man said, grinning down at her. His face shifted between the two she knew, the burn flickering in and out of view. He pushed his hands into the pockets of his labcoat. "Dispose of her," he said, turning away. "The Box should do."

Oumou's breath caught in her chest. She opened her mouth to scream, but no sound came out. The circle of hands grabbed her, wrestling her from her steel bed and forcing her to her feet. In front of her stood a massive vault door. The crank rotated on its own and the door screamed open, its heavy form scraping along the tile floor for what seemed like ages. The darkness of the room stretched out towards her, beckoning her towards its abyss. From inside that inky pit, she heard a wet and ragged breathing sound. It panted expectantly. It wanted her.

Oumou tried to pull her arms free but the hands held her fast. They heaved her into the air and tossed her unceremoniously into the darkness past the portal. Immediately she scrambled to her feet to rush back to the door only for it to slam in her face with a metallic thud.

"No!" She pounded on the door with her fists until they hurt.

With a deep breath, Oumou tried to summon up her powers to tear the door from its hinges, but once again her ears began to ring. The mosquito noise that had been buzzing at the back of her head grew in volume until it felt like her head was going to split open.

The Box was designed to be a punishment room for her: pitch black with a continuous bombardment of painful sound to keep her from focusing. Oumou let out a furious scream and returned to pounding on the door.

"Let me out," she shouted, her knuckles cracking against the solid door. "It was an accident." Her hands screamed with agony, and her arms grew tired. She slumped to the floor, exhausted. Her head throbbed and her eyes burned with the heat of her tears.

She once more became aware of the gasping, sucking sound from the darkest corner of the room. Something shuffled across the floor, hidden in the shadows. It paced the room with a sound like wet flesh slapping on the solid concrete floor. Each step sounded closer and closer until Oumou could smell the thick odor of rot coming off the thing. She pressed her back against the vault door, cold against the sweat permeating through her clothes. The sensation made her shiver. She squinted, willing her eyes to adjust to the darkness, but still couldn't make anything out.

"Who's there?" she asked.

A shuddering gasp emanated from the darkness, followed by a choking, congealed laugh. "Don't you know?" a voice croaked from the darkness. "Don't you remember?"

The thing in the darkness dragged itself into the light, revealing Jim Buckett's dead visage. His corpse climbed out of the darkness, staring at her through milky eyes. The skin on his face hung in loose, pale clumps around a slack jaw that leaked a steady stream of blood. Oumou's scream caught in her throat along with the smell of decaying flesh. She gagged and pressed herself as flat as she could against the vault door. Her whole body trembled.

Broken limbs decorated with protruding bone fragments reached out towards her. Exposed muscle flexed with each motion as the corpse crawled towards her on all fours, grating jagged bone against the concrete floor. The whole body was twisted around on itself, giving it a barely human appearance outside of the sunken face now inches away from hers.

Cold hands thick with congealed blood wrapped their way around her throat, tightening suddenly and forcefully. The air caught in her lungs as her throat filled with the stench of the corpse's foul breath. It rose up on its two broken legs, pulling Oumou up by the throat as it did.

"Killed me," it hissed. "Kill you."

Oumou kicked her feet and grabbed at the thing's hands, sloughing off clumps of skin as she did.

"Kill you!" the corpse screamed. "I'll fucking kill you, bitch!" Blood poured from its mouth down onto her face as it spoke.

Oumou felt the bones in her neck creak under the force until...

"No!" Oumou woke in a frenzy, thrashing and moaning. She gulped down air between hysterical sobs. Amanda bolted upright in the bed and immediately wrapped Oumou in a tight hug.

"It's okay," she said. "It was just a bad dream."

She held Oumou despite her flailing. One of Oumou's elbows caught Amanda in the mouth, splitting her lip and sending a warm trickle of blood down her chin. The blonde girl held fast, rubbing Oumou's back until she calmed down. Oumou blinked away her tears and looked at her friend's bloodied face.

"What happened?" she asked, panic rising again at the sight of blood.

Amanda wiped her face and sucked on the busted lip. "I bit my lip on accident," she said. "Are you okay?"

"Yeah," Oumou said, shakily. "I had a nightmare."

"About the vineyard?"

"Yeah," Oumou said. She didn't mention the dead man.

"You must have been scared," Amanda said, taking Oumou's hand in her own.

Oumou sucked down a huge gulp of air and rubbed her neck. She shuddered at the fading memory of the corpse man. She turned to Amanda with fresh tears in her eyes. "Could...could I have a hug?"

Amanda couldn't contain her smile. "Really?" she asked.

Oumou nodded. "Yes. Please?"

Amanda pulled Oumou into her arms. The warmth she radiated burned in stark contrast to the icy cold of the creature from her nightmare. The warmth comforted her. Her heart began to beat more steadily and the trembling in her arms slowly stopped. She hugged her friend back, and they stayed like that until Amanda drifted back to sleep. Oumou, however, had decided that she would not be returning to the land of nightmares, and instead laid out on her back and counted the cracks in the ceiling, hoping that morning would come around soon.

* * *

The chill of a breeze drifting through an open window caused Oumou to stir.

When did I fall asleep again? she thought. She glanced at the window. *Was that always open?*

Oumou struggled to disentangle herself from Amanda's limbs without waking the girl. She managed to shift around and fully face the window. The eyeless man cut a gloomy figure in the pale moonlight as he stood outside the open window. Oumou noticed with a surge of fear and disgust that patches of flesh all across the man's body looked as though they were burning and festering. In several places, she could see the bones beneath the skin, held in place with deteriorating muscle. He beckoned for her to come outside.

Oumou shook her head furiously.

A smile cracked his skin, sending rivulets of blood running down his face. He nodded and continued to beckon.

Oumou felt her body seized by an invisible force. She was jerked upright and to her feet. "What? No!" Oumou tried to resist but the force was too powerful. With her own power she tried to lock herself in place, yet still her body continued to move towards the open window.

"Welcome," the man said as Oumou climbed out the window and walked to stand in front of him.

"What do you want?" Oumou hissed.

"You will see," he said. "Walk with me."

"I don't want to." Oumou struggled as her feet propelled her after the man as he walked.

"Where are we going?" Oumou asked.

The man did not turn or acknowledge her. Oumou looked up to see the black spires of the town church towering above her. At night the structure looked even more threatening, as though at any moment it might reach down and grab her in obsidian claws, swallowing her up in its infinite darkness.

"No," Oumou whispered. "Not here."

Another smile cracked her companion's face as he gazed down at her. They stopped at the base of the steps leading up to the church's heavy wooden doors. The cold night air whispered through and around Oumou's nightgown. She shivered. Amanda's room had been warm, and she hadn't had time to put anything over top of the thin material. She rubbed her arms in a desperate attempt to warm herself.

"You are strong and willful," he said. "Even now you resist me. You must be broken."

Oumou's head was throbbing from the effort of fighting off the man's control over her. She gasped and gave up. She glared up at the figure next to her. His smile never left his face. He started up the stairs with her in tow. The doors swung open as they approached. Inside the church, shadows danced to the flickering of candles burning in rows alongside the pews. Oumou glanced around nervously as they made their way down the main aisle and up to the lectern. In the low light of the church, she could just make out a shape at the foot of the podium. The man reached down and pulled the fabric away from the form, revealing a swollen face. Oumou flinched at the reveal. Her normal panic did not register. She'd seen worse. She'd done worse.

"Who is he?" she asked.

"Irrelevant," the man said, replacing the covering.

Oumou shivered, but not from the cold. "I don't want to be here." Her eyes darted around, looking for the man in black, half expecting him to emerge from every shadow. She looked up at the man's face. The flickering orange of the candlelight made the dark pits of his eyes seem even deeper. She looked away only to make eye contact with the hanging Jesus sculpture above the lectern. The suffering on his face appeared starker in the strange light. Again, she averted her eyes.

"You are like me," the man said.

"What?"

"You are a monster."

"No, I'm not," Oumou said. "I have a friend, and a family now."

"Is that what you think?" The man walked over to a candle and grasped the flame. He held it, flickering, in the palm of his hand. "That they don't hate you?"

"They don't."

"Since you've arrived, their lives have gotten worse," he said. "They resent you. This whole pathetic little town hates you. And, if push came to shove, they would cast you aside without hesitation." He turned to her, the tiny flame in his hand now a full fireball, highlighting the manic expression on his face. "Like garbage."

"No," Oumou said, "they wouldn't. Amanda wouldn't."

"I'll prove it to you," the man said. The skin on his face burned off, revealing his skull. His teeth clicked as he laughed at her.

The Bibles and hymnals in the room all rose from their cradles and floated towards the man. They drifted through the open flame, igniting completely and circling around him like a burning carousel. Once all of them were lit, the man smirked and clapped his hands together. All at once the fire in his hand vanished and all the burning books shot across the chapel in different directions, colliding with pews and curtains and walls with a shower of sparks before igniting and combining into a massive conflagration. The fire burned so hot that Oumou's nervous sweat dried up almost instantly. Smoke choked her lungs and sent her into a coughing fit. She looked around for the man, but he was gone. She was all alone in the burning church.

The door in the back of the church flung open, slamming into the wall behind it. Oumou's head snapped towards the sound and saw the reverend emerge from his back room.

"What the devil is going on out here?" His eyes locked onto her. "You."

"I didn't—"

"You would come here, into *my* house? You would disrespect me?" he roared.

"It wasn't me!"

She saw the gun before he drew it. Before he could properly aim it, she lashed out with a frustrated scream, sending the reverend to the ground and the gun clattering across the floor.

"The man did it," Oumou said.

Oumou searched around, hoping that the man would appear and reveal himself as the culprit. The hope was stupid, she knew, and it didn't happen. It was just her and the reverend staring each other down at opposite ends of the church.

"All I see is you, girl," the reverend said, clamoring towards the gun, "burning my church." With the gun in hand, he whirled around and fired off a booming shot. The bullet whizzed past Oumou's head, shattering a window behind her.

"Stop it," Oumou said, stomping her foot. The whole church shook with the force of her outburst. The reverend paused and looked towards the ceiling.

"You start a fire and now you threaten to crush me beneath the building," he said. "I'll kill you first." The reverend wiped his eyes as smoke began to make them water. The gun wavered in his hand as he tried to draw a bead on her.

He fired again. The bullet clipped her ear, tearing off a chunk as it went by. Oumou screamed and dropped to her knees. Somewhere overhead, an echoing crack resounded through the church. She looked up at him with tears in her eyes, a growing fury flashing behind them. The barrel of the gun was still aimed at her head. The report of the gun seemed to crack in slow motion. Oumou let a wave of force erupt out of her body, blasting the pews into the walls of the church and shattering them into splinters. The bullet blasted back towards the reverend, ripping through his side and embedding itself in the wall behind him. He crumpled to his knees, clutching his side.

Oumou knew she had to escape. The only place she could think about was the Chastaines' house; Amanda's room and the safety of her bed.

"Damn you," the reverend shouted, forcing himself to his feet.

Oumou bolted to the church's open doors as a bullet struck the place she'd just been. She crossed the threshold to the whiz of another bullet just over top of her head. Her feet pounded down the steps and she sprinted into the street. The gun cracked again and Oumou felt the bullet pierce through her shoulder. Shock stifled her scream as she collapsed to the ground. She struggled to flip over and saw the reverend at the top of the stairs, gun outstretched in one hand, the other still clutching his side that shimmered dark and wet in the glow of the fire.

"Got you, you little bitch," he sneered. He cocked the hammer of the gun again and pulled the trigger. The gun clicked. He pulled the trigger again. Another click. The reverend growled in frustration. He chucked the gun aside and began to descend the steps.

"Stay away." Oumou reached out with her uninjured arm, using all of her power to hold the man in place.

By now a crowd had begun to gather around the spectacle. Oumou looked around for the Chastaines, desperate for their help. She couldn't see any of them among the confused and frightened faces.

A window in the church exploded, and the rush of air reinvigorated the flames, causing them to erupt from every gap, crevice, and portal in the structure like a stonework volcano. Oumou realized too late that the reverend was still in range of the consuming flames. Oumou released him just as the fire swallowed him from behind. The reverend screamed as he stumbled forward away from the flames, toppling down the remaining steps and landing face-first in the dirt.

The crowd began to mutter and point at Oumou, and she realized that, with her hand outstretched and the burning body of the reverend outside the flaming church, it looked very much like she was the one to blame. She looked around at the sea of unforgiving faces before turning back to the reverend. Her blood ran cold. The eyeless man stood over him, looking down on him with a contemptuous grin. Oumou knew that no one else could see him. He didn't want them to. The eyeless man turned his grin on her.

"He's still alive," he said. "Interesting."

Oumou let out a frustrated scream. The whole church creaked and groaned with the force of her rage. The eyeless man scanned the crowd with a widening grin.

"This is perfect," he said. "Now to show you the extent of their hatred." He looked up at the groaning structure of the church. Black shadowy tendrils snaked off his body and wound their way up the church's spire. There was a loud crack as the top of the church was broken away and pulled down towards the ground. The tendrils released the tumbling spire and slithered back into the eyeless man's shadow.

An image of Jim Buckett's corpse flashed in Oumou's mind. She wasn't going to let the reverend die. She didn't want him dead. Blood pooled around her on the ground, spilling more as her pulse quickened. She focused on the falling chunk of rock and caught it, suspending it in the air several feet above the reverend's motionless body. A wave of lightheadedness steamrolled over Oumou as she strained against the weight of the stone.

"Oumou!" Mr. Chastaine's voice cut through the night, startling her.

Her concentration broken, the stone spire slammed into the ground, crushing the reverend beneath it. The sound of cracking stone and crunching bone resounded in the night for a split second before once again falling silent. A thick cloud of dust drifted out from the impact crater.

"No!" Oumou screamed.

Now standing right beside her, the man with no eyes began to laugh. The sound was cruel and hollow, with no warmth whatsoever. "They'll never forgive you for this," he said. "Never. Just you watch."

Oumou slashed at him with her hands only for him to disappear. Rough hands grabbed her by the hair and injured arm, sending searing pain on a surging course through her entire body. The hands jerked her to her feet. Oumou looked up to see the hawk-like eyes of Sylvia Windsor glaring down at her, stormy fury brewing behind her cloudy, unfocused eyes.

"I didn't do it," Oumou whispered.

The woman simply hissed out a laugh in reply.

Oumou tried to wrestle her way out of the woman's iron grip, but the pain in her shoulder was too much. She stopped when her head began to spin.

"Sylvia," Mr. Chastaine said. His eyes wandered from the burning church to the pile of rubble covering the reverend's body before finally settling on Oumou, trapped in the grasp of the angry older woman. "Let her go."

A tense moment of silence passed between the two adults, until finally the woman released her grip. Oumou wobbled as she attempted to make her way over to the man, to the safety he represented. She wanted to sprint, but the thought alone made her dizzy. Instead, she just shuffled forward like a zombie, arms hanging limp at her sides. With her one good arm she reached out a hand for the man.

Mr. Chastaine held up his hand sharply, and she stopped. He crossed the remaining distance to her and knelt down in front of her. His face was stone, and his silence wedged itself in Oumou's heart like a shard of icy steel. He looked at her injury.

"Clean through," he said, matter-of-factly. He tore a bloody strip from the sleeve of her nightshirt and wrapped it around the bleeding hole, pulling it so tight it hurt. Oumou winced at the pain. "You'll live."

"You're a doctor. You'll fix it, right?"

He held her gaze for a moment, his face unreadable. Teri's voice called out to him.

"Harold, what on God's green Earth happened out here?" she asked. "And where's the reverend?"

Oumou looked around at all the expectant faces. She recognized some. Vicki Porter stood aghast. Her thin, pale form glowed a jaundice yellow in the light of the flames. Teri's face was rumpled with concern, her hands wrung tight in front of her bosom. Leah Buckett's eyes were red and swollen, fresh tears still streaming down her face. Oumou felt a pang of guilt. When the woman noticed Oumou staring, the sorrow in her eyes turned to fury. Oumou looked away. Her eyes settled on a face at the very back of the crowd. The man from the church. His dark skin stuck out amongst the sea of pale faces. He nodded as Oumou locked eyes with him. Quick as the gesture was, his eyes immediately returned to scanning the crowd as though he expected the world to fall apart at any minute. He clung to the shadows as he circled around the crowd, slowly making his way closer to the center.

"I don't know," Mr. Chastaine said finally. He turned to the pile of rubble. "But I have a suspicion."

Teri gasped. She looked to the crowd and they muttered their agreement, each telling what they had seen happen. Teri covered her mouth and stared at Oumou. They all did.

"Where's Amanda?" Oumou asked, pulling on Mr. Chastaine's sleeve.

He pulled his hand away. "She's home," he said. "Hopefully still sleeping."

Oumou's heart fluttered. Her friend hadn't seen any of this. She wouldn't hate her. The man was wrong. She opened her mouth to speak.

"But you're not going to see her again," Harold said, his voice uncharacteristically cold.

She felt her heart turn to ice in her chest. Behind her, the fire began to burn out, and the night grew cold once more.

"I don't know *how* all this happened, Oumou." He ran a hand through his hair. "Hell, I'm not sure I even know *what* happened. But you're at the center of it and...look around," he said. "It's too dangerous for Amanda to be a part of." There was sadness in his eyes as he spoke. "I can't put her at risk. She's my daughter."

"But I... But you—"

"My *real* daughter, Oumou," Mr. Chastaine said with a sigh.

Oumou felt the world shatter around her. Tears burned in her smoke-stung eyes, but she refused to let them fall. She blinked them back and stayed silent. Mr. Chastaine kneaded his forehead.

"Can you tell me what happened?" he asked.

"What *happened?*" Sylvia shrieked. She stormed over to Harold and jabbed a crooked finger at the pile of rubble in front of the church. "She burned our church and killed our reverend with her black magic." She wheeled around to face Oumou. "And damn you for it, nigger."

"Sylvia!" Mr. Chastaine's voice boomed in the near silence of the night. The older woman jumped at the sound and regarded him with her lips pursed in disapproval. "Go home. Now."

"You don't tell me what to do, you—"

A gunshot echoed through the night, causing Oumou to flinch. The man from the church shoved his way through the stunned crowd until he stood right next to Mr. Chastaine.

"Evening," he said.

"You?" Mr. Chastaine asked.

"Leslie Johnson. We haven't met, not really."

"I remember you."

"Good, makes this easier," Leslie said. He pointed the gun at Sylvia. "I think he told you to do something, lady." He motioned with the weapon. "Go on now."

Sylvia hissed and slunk away from him and Mr. Chastaine. She glared at Oumou as she passed, but said nothing.

"What are you doing here?" Mr. Chastaine asked.

"First things first," Leslie said, ignoring him. "You may want to take care of that."

The fire had subsided, but it still burned inside the church. Sparks drifted on the wind, threatening to catch on the wooden buildings nearby.

"Right," Mr. Chastaine said. He took a deep breath. "Teri, run and grab Donny. Leah, can you get Jim as well?"

"Jim's dead," Leah said, her words breaking off into a strained sob.

"What?" Mr. Chastaine said, taken aback. "How?" He looked at Teri. "Get Donny," he said, "and be quick, please." He turned his attention back to Leah as Teri jogged off towards Donny's house. "What do you mean he's dead?"

"He told me he had to do a favor for the reverend this morning. Told me not to wait up for lunch. But then he didn't come home for dinner and I got worried so" — she sniffed and wiped her eyes — "I went to talk to the reverend and...and he said that she killed him." Leah pointed her finger directly at Oumou. Ice carved its way through Oumou's veins. She felt cold. Her blood had soaked through the makeshift wrap and stained her nightgown almost entirely red. She tried to say she didn't feel good, but her throat was dry and all she could do was cough.

Mr. Chastaine didn't hesitate. "Leah, that's insane. How could Oumou kill Jim? I mean, look at her." He gestured at Oumou to emphasize his point. "It's not possible."

"Of course you'd defend her," Leah spat. "But ever since she got here, things have been terrible. And now all this? I...I can't be here." She gave Oumou another hateful glare before stalking off in the direction of her home.

Teri returned to the center of the crowd. "Harold, Donny isn't home."

"He's in there," Oumou choked out.

"Damn it," Mr. Chastaine said without looking at her. "All right, all of you get buckets of water and whatever fire extinguishers you have and get to work putting out the rest of the fire." The crowd was slow to disperse, but eventually they moved to action with a quickening pace.

Oumou tugged on Leslie's sleeve once before collapsing to the ground.

"Shit," Leslie said. "Give me a hand."

Mr. Chastaine rushed to Oumou's side and knelt. "She's been shot."

"I can see that now," Leslie shouted.

"Then move, I'm a doctor."

"You should have been focusing on her."

"I got distracted," Mr. Chastaine said.

"Distracted from a little girl with a bullet in her?"

"Things are hectic, and this back and forth is getting us nowhere!" Harold pressed his shirt against the bullet wound. "We need to get her somewhere I can actually look her over."

"Where's your house?" Leslie asked.

"No," Mr. Chastaine said.

"The hell do you mean, 'no'?"

"When that crowd gets back," Mr. Chastaine said, "and finishes with the church, they're going to be out for blood. If she's at my house—"

"Yeah, yeah, I get it," Leslie said. "You got a car?"

"Yes."

"Then I got a place. Hurry up."

Mr. Chastaine hoisted Oumou into his arms as gently as he could. He glanced down at the unconscious girl. "It'll be okay," he said grimly. "I've got you." Then, "I'm sorry." He set off in the direction of home as quickly as he could.

* * *

Leslie directed Harold's drive to the cabin in the forest clearing. The trail wasn't made to be easily accessible by car, so he had to keep a tight grip on Oumou to keep her from spilling onto the floor and worsening her already dire situation. They wound past knotted tree clusters twisted together into gnarled clumps. The car crunched over an exposed root, rattling the passengers and causing Leslie to crack his teeth together.

"Admittedly," he said, "it's a much more pleasant walk."

Harold scowled over the steering wheel. "How much farther?"

"Not too much." Leslie looked down at the girl bleeding out on his coat. "How much of that back there was an act?"

"What are you talking about?"

"You told her she'd never see your daughter again because she was dangerous, but then you stood up for her to everyone. That's dangerous too." Leslie stared at the side of the man's head. "Why risk it?"

"My family is the most important thing to me," Harold said. "They come first."

"But?"

"But what?" Harold snapped.

"There's definitely a 'but' after that sentence."

Harold looked down at Oumou. "But that doesn't mean I don't care about her too." His eyes snapped back to the road as he swerved to avoid a protruding tree stump. "You saw what it was like down there."

"Stage one of a lynching, yeah, I saw."

"I had to play it safe," Harold said.

Finally the trees broke and the clearing opened to reveal the cabin sitting in its middle. Harold threw on the brakes and hopped out of the car, rushing to the passenger side.

"Hand her to me," he said. "Gently, gently."

Leslie slid out of the seat and grimaced at the sight of blood covering his entire outfit.

"Please tell me you're not squeamish," Harold said.

"Seen enough blood," Leslie said. "Never wanted it all over me."

"You get used to it," Harold said.

"I fucking hope not. Door's unlocked." He waved his hand and then stripped out of his coat, tossing it unceremoniously onto the muddy ground.

Harold leaned back out the front door of the cabin. "I need your help in here."

Leslie grimaced again and jogged up the steps. The warmth of the building's furnace was a welcome change of pace from the frigid night air. Leslie stripped out of his suit jacket as well. His white button-down glistened red in dim firelight. "I cleaned up for guests," he said.

Harold laid Oumou out on the table in front of the sofa in the main room. "Turn on the lights," he said.

"Lights don't work," Leslie said. "Blew out a few days ago."

"Flashlight?"

"Furnace," Leslie said. He opened the grate, and the room filled with a flickering red glow. "It's all we got."

"And you *live* here?" Harold asked, ripping through Oumou's nightgown and revealing the puckered bullet wound. "I don't see any bone fragments," he said, grabbing a pair of forceps from his bag. "Hold her down."

"That's good, right?" Leslie did as he was told, careful not to place any pressure on her right side. As Harold entered the wound, checking the damage, Oumou began to struggle and moan.

"Just soft tissue damage. Yes. She'll heal faster."

A stray kick struck Leslie in the ribs.

"Son of a bitch," he said, clamping her leg down against the table. "Isn't she unconscious?"

"Reflex response. And... Okay," he said, dropping the forceps on the table. Oumou still tossed and turned even though the procedure was over. "I'm going to stitch it now. Can you put an IV line in?"

"The fuck do I look like?" Leslie said. "Give me the stitches. Those I can do."

"Right." Harold pulled out a pouch of morphine. The needle went in smoothly, and he pulled it out as he slid the tube into place. He elevated the bag and started the flow. Almost immediately Oumou began to settle. He sighed heavily and sat on the couch. "How are the stitches?"

"They ain't pretty, but the hole's gone," Leslie said. He collapsed on the sofa next to Harold. "Gonna leave a scar too."

"I can't stay too much longer," Harold said.

"You'll break her heart if you aren't here when she wakes up," Leslie said, as he rose and made his way to the kitchen. "Whiskey?"

"I don't drink," Harold said.

"Now's a good time to start." Leslie waggled the bottle back and forth.

"No," Harold said. "Thank you."

"Seriously though, after your little act in the town. If she wakes up with just me here—"

"Make sure to clean the wound frequently. Even with the stitches, there is a chance for infection."

"Don't you change the subject on me," Leslie said, pointing an accusatory finger. "This is important."

"My family is down there in a town that is scared and angry because three people are dead. They don't know exactly what happened, but they think she's involved, and she was staying with my family, which puts them in danger." Harold's voice rose as he spoke, his fists clenching in his lap. "Oumou's condition is stable; my family's circumstances are not."

"You gonna come back after things settle down?"

Harold shook his head. "If she thinks that...that we sent her away, she won't come back. That's what's safest for her. That's for the best."

"The best for who?" Leslie asked. "'Cause it sure as hell isn't for her. Seems very much like it's the best for all those racist motherfuckers down there." He placed the bottle on the table beside

Oumou without taking a drink, then took a breath. "No, you're right. She shouldn't be down there."

"It's not fair," Harold said. "I know. And I wish the world had changed half as much as we act like it did."

"But it hasn't, and we just have to deal," Leslie said. "Go on, then. I'll watch over her."

As Harold was about to leave, Oumou stirred to consciousness. There was a flash of alert panic in her eyes, but it settled when she saw Harold. He went over and knelt down next to her.

"I'm cold," she said, her voice barely a whisper.

"You lost a lot of blood," Harold said. "But you'll be okay."

"Hate me?" she asked.

"No, I just...I don't understand what's going on." Harold squeezed her hand gently. "I have to go now," he said.

Oumou sighed, and her head tilted to the side as she lost consciousness again.

"I'm going now," Harold said. "I can't... I'm trusting you."

Leslie shrugged. "You can still take her with you if you don't."

Harold glanced at Oumou one more time and then left. Leslie slid into the sofa and watched Oumou's shallow breathing. He aired out the wool blanket draped over the back of the couch and placed it over her. For someone that he'd seen crumple a man like a tin can, lying here on the table she looked so frail, so much like a child.

She is *a child*, he reminded himself. *A child with way too much power, in a world that wants her to have none.*

Magnum trotted over and nuzzled his head against Leslie's leg. He let out a soft whimper.

"She'll be all right," Leslie said. "Don't you worry."

* * *

Darkness swam across Oumou's vision. When it cleared, the man from the church was sitting next to her. He absent-mindedly stroked a grey dog that rested its head in his lap.

The man glanced down as she stirred. "You good, kid?"

Oumou felt warm again. She could feel her fingers and toes despite the tingling sensation running through them. Her shoulder throbbed dully. The ceiling above her was unfamiliar. She tried to nod her head but couldn't. She turned her eyes to look at the man.

"Where?" Oumou managed to croak out.

"You're in a cabin. Safe," he said.

"No," Oumou said. "Chastaine?"

"The doctor?" he said. "He had to go back to town. Help with the fire, calm all them motherfu— Calm all them people down."

"Left me?"

The man searched her face. "He saved your life. And then he had to go." He checked the bag connected to her arm, now almost half empty of the clear liquid within. "Halfway there," he said.

"Left me," she repeated.

"Get some more rest. You need it." The man adjusted the blanket on top of her before standing up and moving to a different part of the room.

"Amanda?" she asked.

She couldn't tell if the man responded. Every sound came like a muffled, far away rumble. She watched the liquid drip...drip...drip...

CHAPTER 12

HAROLD CHASTAINE WOKE to the feeling of being poked in the head.

"Dad," Amanda's voice whispered. "Wake up."

He groaned and sat up. "Is this my desk?" he asked, rubbing his eyes. "Did I fall asleep at my desk?"

"Mom said not to wake you up because you were stressed. But I have a question." His daughter bounced on the balls of her feet. She looked at him expectantly.

"Yeah, I guess I am." He sat up and ran a hand through his hair. His vision was blurry, and his eyes stung as he looked around. "What did you need, kiddo?"

"Where's Oumou?" She cocked her head to the side. "When I woke up, she wasn't there anymore."

Harold hesitated in his response. "Oumou...had to leave."

"Where did she go?"

"She's okay, sweetie, I—"

Amanda crossed her arms and began to pout angrily. "You said she could stay with us."

"Amanda, Oumou couldn't stay here anymore. People think she did something really bad." Mr. Chastaine placed his hands on her shoulders. "But she's okay."

"Oumou wouldn't do anything bad." Amanda pulled away from her father. "She's nice."

"I had to send her somewhere safe," Harold said. "Do you understand?" Harold realized his mistake as soon as the words left his mouth.

"You sent her away?" Amanda said, her face rumpling in thought. "But she was my friend..."

"Honey—"

"She was my best friend, and you sent her away!" Amanda screamed. "Why are you so mean?"

Elizabeth swept into the room and scooped Amanda into her arms. "Oh, sweetie," she said, "your dad isn't being mean. He was trying to help Oumou."

"Why couldn't he help her here?" Amanda stomped her foot. "With us."

Harold rubbed his eyes and looked at the clock on the wall. It was early. He'd apparently only managed two hours of sleep. That explained the pounding in his head. "I did what I had to do," Harold said, harsher than he meant. He softened his tone. "I had to."

"But we said we'd help her," Amanda carried on, "and now she thinks we hate her!"

A pang of guilt stabbed at Harold's conscience. That was exactly what Leslie Johnson had said. He took a deep breath. "But she's safe," he said. "She couldn't stay here."

By the time he'd returned, the fire had died down, but passions were burning even hotter. In his absence, Sylvia and Leah had whipped the crowd into a frenzy, blaming Oumou for every death and a handful of other even more ludicrous activities. Half of the town had gone for their guns, while the other half had armed themselves with whatever they could find. Only Vicki and Teri had stayed out of it, off to the side and out of the way of Sylvia's wrath. When Harold had tried to calm the crowd, she chucked a piece of rubble at his head, barely missing.

Placating an angry mob, he thought, *really isn't in my job description.*

"Dad?" Amanda asked. "What're you staring at?"

"Huh? Oh, sorry, sweetie, I must have zoned out." Harold sat back in his chair and forced a soft chuckle.

"You don't think Oumou did anything bad, do you?"

"No, I just...I don't really know what happened, and that's what I'm going to try to figure out." He rose from his chair. "I tried calling the next town over to see if they could spare any officers, but it seems they're in the midst of dealing with a mass murderer, so they won't be any help." He looked at his wife. "I told Dave about Jim and all he asked was, 'Did Leah do it?'"

"Asshole," Elizabeth said. "Sorry, sweetie." She tousled a giggling Amanda's hair.

The little girl broke free of her mom's hold and gave a small, excited jump. "So I can go visit her?"

"Who?"

"Oumou!"

"No," Harold said at the same time as his wife.

The little glimmer of happiness curdled back into hurt-fueled anger. "Why not?"

"It's not safe," her mom said.

"But Oumou is safe!" She stomped her foot. "You just said she didn't do anything bad!"

"Kiddo," Harold said in a weary voice, "I know Oumou protected you from the bad guys before. But the people in this town are scared. If they find out you're visiting her..." His voice broke. "I just want *you* to be safe, okay?"

"Once Daddy gets this all sorted, we can go see Oumou. How about that?" her mother added. She shot a silencing look at Harold. "Right?"

"Of course," Harold said. He didn't know if he was lying or not.

"Okay," Amanda said. She thought for a moment, knitting her brow. "I guess." She rocked back and forth on her heels. "Can I go see Ms. Vicki instead? I want to borrow a book to read while I wait."

"I don't know if that's the best—"

"Harold Chastaine," Sylvia's piercing voice called from outside their front door.

"Hold that thought," Harold said, his face darkening.

He opened the door and stood face to face with Sylvia. She'd seen better days. Her hair, normally perfectly brushed, was full of flyaway hairs. Whatever makeup she wore she'd slept in, leaving dark circles around her eyes. Her beady eyes darted around behind him, probably looking for Oumou, he thought.

"Here to throw another rock at my head?" Harold said bitterly.

"Where is she?" Sylvia hissed.

"Leslie took her."

"Where?"

"Don't know. And I wouldn't tell you anyway," Harold said. "Is this why you came here?"

Sylvia's lips pursed and curled down into a scowl. "The town wants answers," she said. "They want to know what happened. They demanded you." Disgust creeped across her face. Harold knew he wasn't who she wanted taking charge.

"That was my plan anyway," Harold said. "You didn't need to come get me."

"Enough of this," she snapped. "Are you ready to go or not?"

"One minute," Harold said, closing the door in her face. He walked back over to Amanda and his wife.

"Your mom and I are going to go into town and make sure everything is all right," he said, patting Amanda on the head. "You can head over to Ms. Vicki's house, and stay there and read until we come get you, okay? Tell Ms. Vicki we owe her a wine night."

"Okay," Amanda said, a smile glowing on her face. "See you later!"

Harold flashed a tired smile in response to hers. "Go straight to Ms. Vicki's house, okay?" He opened the door for her, ignoring Sylvia's sputtering indignation.

"I know." Amanda skipped past the grey-haired woman with a wave and made her way down the street. "I wonder what I'll read," she said loudly.

"I have to get my medical examination kit," Harold said, closing the door once more.

"You're being awfully rude to her," Elizabeth said.

"She threw a chunk of rock at my head," Harold said. "She's lucky my oath keeps me from doing her any harm, like, say, an incorrect dose of morphine?"

"Harold!"

"Just a bit of dark humor. My head is killing me." He grabbed the bag off his office desk and slung it over his shoulder. "You ready?"

"Yeah," Elizabeth said. She took his hand in hers.

Sylvia was still waiting when they opened the door, her face a bright crimson. She opened her mouth to speak.

"Sorry about the wait," Harold said. "I just woke up."

"It doesn't matter," she said.

"Where to?" he asked.

"The church," she said. "I want to know *how* she killed the reverend."

Harold stopped. "Sylvia, as a licensed doctor I can safely say that the reverend died from the chunks of rock that fell on him, so please, don't come here spouting some ridiculous fantasy."

Sylvia scowled. "You'll see," she said.

* * *

There wasn't much to be done about the reverend's body until the rubble could be cleared, so Harold decided to start inside the church, where Oumou said Donny had been. The body lay at the foot of the lectern, naked and burned so much that Harold couldn't be sure it really was Donny. He prodded the body with a pen.

"Well," Harold said. "He was dead before the fire."

"And how would you know that?" Sylvia said.

"I don't know many people who would just lay out in the middle of a fire," Harold said. "That and, from what I can make of the face, there's no sign of distress or agony. He wasn't aware that he was burning."

"Can you tell how he died?"

"He wasn't shot," Harold said. "My best guess is still some sort of asphyxiation, though" — he leaned in closer, holding his breath — "his jaw appears to be broken. So blunt force trauma is also a possibility."

"The poor boy," Sylvia said. "Taken from us too soon."

"He was thirty, and he made his own choices," Harold said.

"You think he deserved this?"

"I think that following a bad person often leads to a bad end."

Sylvia's face twitched with anger. "What are you implying?"

Harold ignored her and pried open the corpse's mouth. "Teeth are missing, no, wait" — he reached with a pair of tweezers and pulled out a tooth — "he swallowed them. Someone beat him bad," Harold said. "Jim, maybe? Seems he has a penchant for hitting things."

Sylvia inched closer, leaning in to look at the body.

Harold rolled his eyes and sighed. "What is it, Sylvia?"

"Is there anything...strange...about the body?" she asked.

"Strange how?" Harold said.

"Supernatural?" Sylvia said. "Evil?"

"A man was murdered. I think that constitutes evil, don't you?" He stood up. "I'm no detective, but based on the location of the body, the fact that he appears to have been beaten or choked to death, and the subsequent fire..." Harold sighed. This was not going to go over well. "It looks like the reverend killed him and burnt down the church, possibly to frame Oumou."

Sylvia sucked in a raspy breath.

Here it comes, Harold thought.

"You would cast aspersions on our late reverend? Besmirch his good name to defend that devil child?" Her eyes bulged wildly as she went on her tirade. Harold didn't have the energy to stop her.

"Like I said, that's just what it looks like to me," Harold said. "Everything is so damn up in the air, but come on, you saw how the reverend treated Donny."

"Like a kicked puppy," Elizabeth said.

"And like it or not," Harold continued, "it's far more plausible than an eleven-year-old being some kind of...supernatural killer."

"Witchcraft has been around since the Old Testament," Sylvia said. "Its practitioners have always stood as defiant abominations in the eyes of the Lord."

Harold ignored the statement. "What I don't get is why you weren't surprised when I said how I thought he died. Sylvia, if you know something—"

"What I know is that that girl is evil and you two are consorting with her and can't be trusted!" She backed her way down the main aisle of the burned-out church, stumbling over charred chunks of wood and stone. "You are a liar!" she shrieked. "The reverend only ever did what was best for you and the rest of these ungrateful sinners."

"Is it just me," Harold said, "or has she gotten crazier since Sunday?"

"Do you think *she* did it?" Elizabeth asked.

"She definitely knows more than she's letting on," he said, "which makes her calling me a liar kind of funny, in an ironic sort of way, don't you think?"

"She's a horrible, miserable old woman," Elizabeth said. "But I don't know if she's crazy enough to murder a person."

Outside of the church, Sylvia let out a hair-raising screech before trickling off into a mad cackle. "Yes," she screamed. "Yes!"

"Maybe I spoke too soon," Harold said, snatching up his medical bag and rushing outside. "What the hell are you screaming about?" He came to a stop behind Sylvia.

She had fallen to her knees and was gazing, glassy-eyed, at the pile of black stone that once had been the church's steeple. A maniac smile knifed its way across her face as she kneaded her hands together.

"He is risen," she said, cackling.

"Full disclosure," Harold said, "she is really starting to piss me off."

"She's frightening," Elizabeth said.

Sylvia laughed again, gripping her sides until tears ran down her face. "And the stone of the tomb was rolled away, and inside there was no body!" she said, raising her hands to the sky.

Despite his feelings about the woman, Harold was still a doctor. He knelt down beside her and placed a calming hand on her shoulder. "What's wrong, Sylvia?" he asked.

"Nothing," she said. "Everything is right. See for yourself." She pointed an arthritic finger at the pile of rubble.

Harold looked at the rubble for the first time since he passed it that morning. His blood ran cold in his veins. What had once been a pile of rubble was now a neatly arranged circle of black stone with an empty clearing in the middle. There was no blood on the ground or on the stones. And there wasn't a body.

"Where's the reverend's body?" Harold said, the first tinges of panic creeping their way into his voice. "What type of sick game is this?"

Sylvia let out a hyena laugh. "No games, just divine providence."

"Did you do this?" Harold asked. "*How* did you do this?"

The rocks were too big for Sylvia to have moved on her own, and the blood from the body had definitely been there when they'd entered the church earlier. For her to move the stones and the body and clean up in that short amount of time was impossible. Doubly so for the frail lunatic in front of him.

"The Lord has given our dear reverend a second chance to complete the work that he started. He looked upon it and declared that it was good."

There's no way he survived the rockfall. Harold's mind raced. *She couldn't have spirited the body away. It's impossible. So then how—*

Sylvia grabbed Harold by the collar and pulled his face down until it was right in front of hers. He could smell ointment and talcum powder as she spoke.

"That little bitch is going to get what's coming to her," she hissed through clenched teeth. "Just you wait." She pushed him away and began to laugh and praise once more.

Harold stumbled back and brushed off his sweater. He tried to look calm, but panic was pounding at the inside of his chest. *Breathe*, he thought. But the panic was too much. He could hear his pulse in his ears.

"Oumou!" he shouted finally. "Elizabeth, stay here and don't let her hurt herself. I have to go." He set off running towards their house.

"Absolutely not," Elizabeth said, following him. "I'm coming with you."

CHAPTER 13

VICKI PORTER PAUSED her reading of the leather-bound book of poetry on her lap when the first knock echoed softly through her house. She waited a moment, and then began reading again. A second knock came, and Vicki sighed, closing the book and setting it on the small table next to her armchair, and made her way to the front door. She checked the peephole. The crown of a small head covered in curly blonde hair just barely peeked into her field of view.

Vicki looked back at the book on the arm table with a sigh. "Later, Sappho," she said.

"Ms. Vicki!" Amanda called from outside. "I came to borrow a book. Dad wanted to get me out of the house because Ms. Sylvia showed up to talk to him. Can you please let me in?"

Vicki smiled to herself and rolled her eyes. She opened the door and looked down into Amanda's beaming face. "Hello there," she said. "You walked all the way out here by yourself?"

"Yep!" Amanda rushed forward and wrapped her arms tight around Vicki's waist. "Hi!"

Vicki patted the girl on the back and said, "You said you wanted to borrow a book?"

"Well..." Amanda said, releasing Vicki from her bear hug and walking into the house. "Kind of." She plopped down in the armchair and glanced over at the book. "What's this?"

"It's a book of love poems," Vicki said. "I don't think it's the kind of book you'd be interested in."

"Maybe when I'm older?"

"Maybe," Vicki said. "Would you like some cookies and milk?"

"Yes, please," Amanda said, springing from the chair and bouncing up and down.

"Kitchen table then," Vicki said, making her way to the cupboard. She pulled out a package of Oreos and set them on the table. A few seconds later a tall glass of milk appeared next to the cookies. Amanda split her first Oreo in half and licked out the filling. Then she dunked the two cookie pieces into the milk and ate them in one quick bite.

"Now, was there a particular book you wanted?" Vicki dunked her own cookie and took a bite from it. She popped the second half in her mouth before picking out another one.

"It's not actually for me," Amanda said sheepishly.

"Let me guess," Vicki said with a soft smile, "it's for Oumou, isn't it?"

"Everyone thinks she did something bad, but she's good. Do you think she did something bad?"

"I think the people in town are scared and they want someone to blame. And their prejudices fuel that fear and turn it to hate." Vicki remembered the anger of the crowd the night before. She and Teri had been afraid that the mob might turn on them right then and there.

"I think Oumou is scared too," Amanda said.

"I'm sure she is," Vicki said. "So then, what book did you want to take to her?"

"I know the book, but I can't give it to her."

"Why not?"

"Dad said I can't see Oumou, because it's not safe." Amanda scuffed the heel of her shoe against the wooden floor. "I was hoping you would take it to her for me?"

Vicki was taken aback. "I'm sorry?"

"I was thinking that since I can't go, you could take the book to her for me? Because you don't think she did anything bad. And I know just the book!"

"Well, I don't know—"

"Please?" She drew out the word and clamped her hands together like she was praying.

"Well, for starters, I don't even know where she is. Your dad took her away with that journalist." Vicki nervously nibbled on her Oreo and adjusted her glasses.

"But Dad says you know *everything* about the town. You'd be able to figure out where he might have taken her, right?" Amanda's eyes lit up with excitement. "Please say you'll do it!"

"That's very kind of your dad to say, but no one knows everything about anything. I just try to learn and keep track of as much as I can." She glanced at Amanda's puppy dog eyes and sighed. There was nothing more stubborn than a child with its mind made up.

"I guess we could look over some maps and see if something sticks out," Vicki said.

"Really?" Amanda said, leaping to her feet and hugging Vicki from the side. "Thank you! Thank you! Thank you!"

"There's no guarantee we'll find anything, you know? Don't thank me now just to start crying later," Vicki said sternly.

"I won't cry," Amanda said.

Vicki headed to her study, sliding open the double doors and looking around. The study could operate as a library in its own right. The room, which was most likely meant to be the master bedroom originally, was full of floor to ceiling bookshelves which were each in turn filled with books of all kinds, sizes, and colors. Not even the floor avoided the creeping advance of large stacks of books in grave danger of toppling over. Vicki waded through the stacks like a mouse in the maze it now called home. Despite the apparent disorganization, Vicki knew exactly where everything was, and every item in the room had its place.

"Now you stay—"

Amanda skipped into the study and immediately started touching and grabbing at books and maps, flipping through them and then leaving them wherever she left them, and not, Vicki thought bitterly, where they belonged. With a sigh, Vicki made her way to the desk in the far corner of the room and opened up a drawer, pulling out an armful of large rolled-up sheets of paper. She could always fix the mess later.

"These are the maps?" Amanda questioned.

"Yes," Vicki said. "Of the town."

"They look old."

"Some of them are very old." She noticed that Amanda did not seem to understand the point of the older maps. "We can look and see if there are any good places for Oumou to hide. Things that might not be on newer maps"

"Oh!" Amanda said, scurrying over and knocking over a stack of books in the process. Vicki winced, but said nothing at the destruction of her chaotic organization. The blonde girl plopped down into the desk chair and shifted the papers and other objects away from the center. Vicki let out a soft whine but spread the first map out in the now empty space.

"You can put the maps here now," Amanda said.

"Yes," Vicki said, "of course." She glanced across the room at an empty table which she had specifically designated for map use. The first map took up the entire center of the desk when she unrolled it.

"So that's the church, right?" Amanda said, pointing to a rectangle marked with a single cross. "Which makes this my house!" She drew a diagonal line with her finger across the town to a much smaller rectangle.

"This entire map is of just the town of Archwood, actually," Vicki said. She scanned the piece of paper. "It doesn't even have my house on it now that I look closer, so I'm not sure it will help us, since Oumou most likely isn't in the town anymore." She glanced down at Amanda, whose face dropped at the statement. The maps rustled around in her arms until she found the one she was looking for. She rolled up the map on the desk and put it to the side, replacing it with the new map.

"This one's all yellow," Amanda said.

"It's older," Vicki responded. "Probably the oldest one I have." Her eyes roamed the map, stopping on an empty clearing in the forest. "Now that's interesting."

"What?" Amanda practically pressed her face into the map.

"This clearing," Vicki said. She rolled out another map on top of the old map. The clearing was still there, but now there was a symbol representing a house right in its center. Vicki tapped the house symbol and said, "That would be close enough, but reclusive enough that no one would think to look for it."

"Is that where Oumou is?"

"It's a very good guess," Vicki said.

"So, yes?"

"So, maybe."

"Are you going to go?" Amanda was rocking excitedly in the desk chair, a wide smile on her face.

Vicki pinched the bridge of her nose. "I suppose."

Amanda squealed. "Thank you so much, you're the best!" She jumped up and headed for the door. "Make sure to tell her I miss her."

"Amanda!" Vicki called.

The young girl skidded to a halt. "Yes?"

"You never told me what book to give her."

"My favorite one!" she said. She grinned from ear to ear.

Vicki returned the smile. "Of course."

Amanda bounded out of the house, saying "thank you" before closing the door behind her. Vicki sighed, slumping into the desk chair. She sifted through the now disorganized array of papers and books on the desk. She opened one of the drawers and pulled out the copy of the book she kept there to easily grab whenever Amanda decided that she wanted to read it again. The pages rustled as she flipped through them with an amused smile. She closed the book and slipped it into her purse. It fit easily. The map did not fit. With a frustrated sigh, Vicki pored over the map, forcing herself to commit it to memory. Luckily, the clearing wasn't too far from her home via her backyard.

Vicki pulled on her shawl and grabbed her car keys. "It's no good for you to be walking through a forest without a map, V," she said to herself. "Plus, you'll want to be back before nightfall." She looked out the window at the sun, now almost fully overhead in the sky. "All right."

Vicki placed the map on the seat next to her and checked her mirrors before starting the car and pulling off towards a marked path that looked wide enough to accommodate her car. Given the distance, it shouldn't take her more than an hour to reach her destination. She pulled the book out of her purse and set it on top of the map, taking in the bright green cover.

"*Frog and Toad*," Vicki said with a soft chuckle. "If that isn't Amanda, I don't know what is."

CHAPTER 14

OUMOU WOKE TO the familiar, mouth-watering smell of bacon. In her short time at the Chastaines' it had quickly become her favorite food. Her eyes still stung from last night's smoke. She rubbed at them, which made them water as well. Something warm and wet lapped at her elbows. She opened her eyes and looked down to see a grey dog's amber eyes looking back up at her. Its tongue lolled out of its mouth and licked her arm one last time. Magnum barked and wagged his tail back and forth rapidly. He spun around in front of her, barked again and returned to his tail wagging.

"Bark to you too," Oumou said with a warm smile. "Where am I?"

The third bark, while still friendly and excited, was less than helpful at answering her question. Oumou slid from under the heavy wool quilt and felt the cold shock of her bare feet on the hardwood floor. The smell wafted from the kitchen, and she could hear movement from there as well. She tried her best to be quiet as she tip-toed to the kitchen door and cracked it open. She peaked around the corner. The man at the stove was tall, and thin as a straw. His thinning hair was cropped short with distinguished waves running horizontally across his scalp. He was the only person Oumou could remember seeing with skin darker than hers.

Magnum announced her spying with a loud bark and pushed past her. The door swung wide open with a loud, drawn out creak. The man turned to her and waved with the spatula, and she stood there frozen with embarrassment at being caught. He laughed at her.

"The look on your face," he said. He rubbed Magnum on the head and dropped a piece of bacon into the dog's waiting mouth.

"You were there last night," she said. "I," she looked embarrassed, "don't remember your name."

"You were bleeding out," he said. "I think I can forgive you for not remembering my name. It's Leslie. Leslie Johnson."

Oumou nodded. "Thank you for helping me, Mr. Johnson."

"No, no. Nope. None of that," he said. "Call me Leslie. Mr. Johnson is dead in the ground, and hopefully a hell of a lot deeper than that." He finished the sentence with a lower voice than he started, hoping she wouldn't hear.

"Okay," Oumou said. "Where are we?"

"Somewhere safe. At least from the townsfolk." Leslie slid a plate of bacon and eggs onto the rickety looking table. "You've gotta be hungry. Eat up."

"Am I...trapped here?" Oumou asked. She tried to hide the longing glance that she gave the plate of food.

"Well, you can leave," Leslie said, "but I don't suggest it. You're not a prisoner, if that's what you're asking."

"Okay..." she said.

"The food's safe," Leslie said. "Why would I save you just to hurt you?"

"You don't think I killed the reverend, do you?" she blurted out.

"Preacher man? No," Leslie said. "We both know who did that, don't we? That other guy though...you messed him up real good."

Oumou averted her eyes. "I didn't mean to."

"No shame in that," Leslie said. "Self-defense, pure and simple. But no, I know you didn't kill the reverend."

"You could see him?"

"The King of Thorns?"

"The man with no eyes?"

Leslie switched off the stove and sat down at the table holding a second plate. He whistled breathily. "I don't know much, kid, but that ain't no man."

"But he looks like a man?" Her eyes burned, but there was no smoke. She felt anger begin to boil inside of her. "What does he want from me?"

Leslie rocked back in the chair and put his feet up on the table, just far enough away from his plate to ensure none of the previous night's dirt accidentally seasoned his eggs. "You Christian?" Leslie asked.

"I don't know."

"You go to church?" he clarified.

"Once."

"Oh. Right." Leslie massaged his forehead. "Anyway, we got these things called demons. Nasty little bastards. Thing is, they got this ability: they can possess people."

"Possess?" Oumou didn't know the word.

"Yeah, possess. Like, control you. Take over. Own. They can own you," Leslie said. "That's why it looks like a person, and that's what it wants."

"To own me..." Oumou thought. "Why?"

"Well, you're the girl who can snap every bone in a man's body with her mind. Or *not* drop a church on a guy's head. It wants a helping of that power to add to its own." He sat forward in the chair. "Use yours to destroy the world."

Ice filled her veins as she imagined herself, eyeless and cruel, doing to the Chastaines what she did to Jim Buckett. "I don't want to hurt anyone," Oumou said.

"Would that I could do what you do," Leslie mused. "There'd be a lot of dead racist motherfuckers around." He froze. "Ah shit, I'm trying not to cuss around you, but I keep forgetting."

"I don't mind," Oumou said, not really knowing what he was talking about. "You would purposely hurt people with my powers?"

"Yes. No. Maybe. Look, what I'm trying to say is, it's not your fault, kid. You were scared and you defended yourself. Happens to everyone." He looked like he was going to reach across the table and put a hand on her shoulder, but stopped and started to eat his breakfast instead. Oumou became painfully aware that she hadn't started on hers either.

She scarfed down the meat noiselessly, saving a single piece for last, and then set to work on the eggs. Magnum sat at her feet expectantly. He panted loudly, and stared so hard it was obvious that he wanted a portion of her breakfast. Oumou looked solemnly at her single remaining bacon strip. She scowled at the dog, tore off a piece of the meat, and tossed it to him.

"That's all you get," she said.

After a measure of silence broken only by the scraping of utensils on plates, Leslie spoke up. "You know, I'm kind of like you...not the same, but similar."

Oumou's head shot up. There had been no one else like her at the lab. "What?"

"I can see things," he said, "things that have happened, and things that might happen." He rubbed his head. "It's nowhere near as impressive, but—"

"Can you show me my parents?" Oumou asked, without hesitation. "From before all of this?"

Leslie's eyes narrowed. "What do you mean?" He plucked his last cigarette from his jacket pocket and stuck it in his mouth. "Goddamn," he said. "No light."

"I don't remember what they look like," she said. "Just the lab. Can you show me them?"

Leslie tucked the cigarette back in his pocket with a sigh. "I'm not sure—"

"You can see things that happened, right? I want to know why they let the people take me and experiment on me," Oumou said.

Leslie's eyes widened, obviously taken aback. He sucked his teeth. "Sorry, it don't work like that." He rubbed the coarse stubble that covered his jawline. "Plus, I never tried it with more than one person."

"Please, I...I need to know. Amanda and her family were so nice but...my family."

"I said it doesn't work like that."

"Can you try?" Oumou said.

"Kid..." Leslie moved to the sofa and patted the adjacent cushion for her to sit next to him. "I don't think I can."

Oumou plopped down and looked up at him with her best pleading look. When she saw that he didn't respond to puppy dog eyes, her face turned downcast instead.

"Look," he said, "my power only works when I'm asleep and I can't really control it. I don't know how."

"I won't get to see them again," Oumou said, staring at a faded stain on the floor. "Ever?"

He sucked his teeth again. "Damn it. Okay, I may have done a little bit of research when I first started having the dreams, so...I may have an idea. But it could be dangerous. You sure you want to?"

Oumou nodded vigorously. "I need to know."

Leslie returned it with a solemn nod. "You may not feel that way after you find out. Take it from me, some things are better off staying in the past."

He stood and crossed to where his long jacket hung on a mounted hook on the wall. Oumou watched as he fished around in the pockets. A few seconds later he returned with a small cylindrical container and held it in front of her face. "You know what these are?"

"No."

"It's a medicine to put people to sleep." He rattled the little white pills in their case like a prescription maraca. "I've occasionally used them to force out a dream when I needed to find a good story."

"You're going to take them?"

"We both are," he said. "If you want."

Oumou slid away from Leslie and eyed him suspiciously. "Why would I take them?"

"I read a book on voodoo—"

"That sounds like a made-up word," Oumou scoffed.

"All words are made up when you think about it," Leslie said. "Now, do you want to have a chance at seeing your parents or not?"

"I do," she said. "Sorry."

"Right. Anyway, in this book it said that witch doctors could enter people's minds by placing them in a trance and then entering a trance themselves. Always wondered if my power worked the same, but never had a reason to try until now."

He noticed the skeptical look still plastered on her face.

"Up to you. No pressure," he said. "But this is the only way I can think to show you."

Oumou thought for a minute. "You take them first."

"Fair enough." Leslie shrugged, screwed off the cap and popped a pill in his mouth. He washed it down with a swig of whiskey. "See you on the other side," he said. "Or if not, at least I'll be well-rested." He shooed her off the couch and laid down across its length, fluffing a dusty throw pillow up under his head. "Don't forget to take it with water," he said. "You won't see shit if you choke to death. Plus, they taste nasty as hell."

"You didn't use water."

"Suit yourself." Within a matter of minutes, he was snoring. Oumou watched him for a while, making sure he wasn't trying to trick her, that he wouldn't open his eyes after she took the medicine and haul her off to another lab. She poked his face, shouted, and shook him. He didn't stir, just snored. Loudly, she noticed.

She decided he wasn't about to wake up anytime soon, so she pulled out a pill herself. She popped it in her mouth and tried to swallow, but it got stuck. A bitter taste filled her mouth and she could feel the pill lodged in her throat. She ran to the kitchen in a panic and filled a glass with water, choking it down in huge gulps. The pill dislodged, and while the taste didn't vanish, its lingering assault on her taste buds was far less aggressive. She filled the glass up again and drained that just as quickly. She carried the empty glass back out to where Leslie slept. She sat down in front of the couch and waited. A warm, fuzzy feeling began to bloom in her chest, spreading out into her limbs until her whole body tingled. Worry flared up in her mind.

Did he trick me?

But soon she began to relax. She lay down on the floor with her arms and legs spread. Her breathing slowed, coming in long, even intervals. The wood around her felt like the down pillows of Amanda's bedroom. It felt like she was sinking into the pillows, deeper and deeper. Her eyelids grew heavy. She rolled over onto her side and tucked her hands under her head. Heavy eyelids drooped closed, plunging her into darkness.

* * *

She was in the cabin. *They* were in the cabin. She looked to her right and Leslie was there. His arms were folded across his chest.

"Took you long enough," he said.

Oumou looked around the cabin. Everything looked the same, but some things were slightly different. The lights were on and the dust that seemed to cling to every surface was nowhere to be found. It felt warm and inviting. The air smelled of cranberries. They were in the cabin, but it no longer seemed to be abandoned.

"Did they work?" Oumou asked. "Why are we still here?"

"You ever have a nightmare where you dream that you're in your bed?" Leslie asked.

"No. I dream about the lab."

"Okay, I don't know how to address that statement," Leslie said. "Point is, every dream has a hub world of sorts. The place the dream starts. Look closer."

Oumou did. Everything was steeped in the surreal tinge of dream fog. Hazy particles drifted through the air, always floating just out of view when she tried to focus on them. She reached out a hand to touch the wall. Her hand stopped at the wall, but she couldn't feel it at all.

"So since we fell asleep in the cabin...?"

"Exactly."

"Well, what do we do?" Oumou asked.

"Your past, your lead," Leslie said, gesturing at the vaguely shifting room with his hand. "What do we do?"

Oumou thought for a moment, scanning the room for anything that seemed to stand out. She noticed a trapdoor in the floor.

"Food cellar," Leslie said.

Oumou took a step forward. The door flew open as she approached it.

"This way," she said, making her way to the hidden passage.

Leslie followed her to the steps with a sarcastic eye roll. "Yeah, the secret passage swinging open as you approach might just be a tell-tale sign of where to go."

As they descended into the darkness, the air changed from the dank heavy musk of a sealed basement to a cool night breeze with a subtle smell of maple. The darkness of the cellar gave way to a moonlit forest cast in shadow by the warm light emanating from the cabin. Crickets chirped noisily, and off in the distance Oumou could just make out the sad hoot of an owl. The stairs into the cellar had led them to the edge of the forest clearing, facing towards the cabin they had been in not thirty seconds earlier.

"Inside leads to outside," Leslie said. He reached into his pocket for his flask and came up with nothing. "Damn dream logic."

"Someone's coming out," Oumou said.

The door to the house opened and the warm orange light spilled out into the grassy clearing. A well-built black man exited, a slight tremble in his step. His checkered button-down shirt was darkened with sweat. Square glasses repeatedly slipped down a face slick with nervousness. His face was the perfect picture of concern.

"Listen now, we don't want any trouble," he said, projecting his voice.

"How can he see us?" Oumou asked

"Uh," Leslie said, turning Oumou around by her shoulder. "He's not talking to us."

From the darkness the forest came alive with the light of torches. Several figures clad in long white robes emerged from the shadows of the forest. The glow of fire cast shadows on their masks, deepening the shadows that their masks cast over their eyes. They came forth, one figure became ten, became twenty, became fifty, all approaching the man and his house.

The man from the cabin shivered, but it was apparent the cold was not the reason he shook. To his credit, he tried his best to look tough and unperturbed. He puffed out his chest and folded his arms across it.

A woman's voice called from inside the house. "Jeremiah?"

"Stay inside, Simone," he replied, not taking his eyes off the surrounding figures. "It's not safe out here."

"No, you don't understand," the woman named Simone continued, rushing to her husband's side. "I can't find Oumou!"

At the mention of her name, Oumou felt like she'd been struck by lightning. Her whole body vibrated with a palpable energy. The man's look of fear clamped down on her heart like a vice. His head swiveled back and forth, looking for her.

"Where did you last see her?" he asked.

"She asked if she could play in the forest. I told her to stay close."

"The forest?" His head snapped back towards the approaching men, and his face dropped.

"Oh my god," Simone said, clasping her hands in front of her mouth.

A robed figure stepped forward, clutching a small child by the straps of a pair of denim overalls. The girl, no more than three, swung about, shouting and flailing. Oumou recognized herself immediately.

"No, please," Jeremiah said. "Don't."

"This doesn't look good," Leslie said. "Maybe we should—"

"That's me," Oumou whispered. "And those are...my parents."

"And that's the Klan," Leslie hissed. He reached down and pinched Oumou on the arm. "We should go." He pinched himself next. "Ah, damn it."

Oumou gasped in pain and rubbed her arm. "What?"

"We need to wake up," Leslie said.

"No. I need to know what happened."

Leslie glanced from Oumou to her parents to the mob forming around them. He thought about Oumou and Amanda being attacked in the vineyard and his heart sunk. The outcome of the night was becoming clearer by the second. It occurred to him that he'd never considered whether or not a dream could kill him until now. He shook off the thought. "We die, this is on you." He kneaded his temples. "I'm bantering with a child. Fuck."

The Klansmen approached. The one with Oumou in his grip was draped in a blood-red robe. He tossed her to the ground at her father's feet. Before the man could react, Simone rushed out to scoop her daughter up in her arms and retreat back behind her husband. Her eyes were wide with terror.

"Get into the house," Jeremiah said. He held up his arms to block her from the Klansmen, and slowly backed towards the open door as his wife and child hurried inside. The red-robed man stepped forward and grabbed Jeremiah by the collar of his shirt.

"You know why we're here," he said.

"We have nowhere else to go. This is our only home." Jeremiah pulled himself free and got down on his knees and clasped his hands, a desperate man praying to a cruel, unforgiving god. "Just let us be. We don't want any trouble."

"You asked for trouble when you decided to come here. You practically *begged* for it when you spread your seed."

The circle tightened around the lone man. He began to plead again but was cut off by the red-robed man holding up a hand. "Don't diminish your kind further by begging," he said. A roar of laughter rose up from the mob. Jeremiah hung his head.

Oumou didn't see who threw it, but the first blow landed with a sickening crunch she could hear from across the clearing. Oumou's jaw tightened as her mother screamed from inside the house.

Taking turns laughing, kicking, stomping, and punching, the Klan took their time enjoying every bone that snapped, every tooth sent flying, and every muffled exclamation of pain. They reveled in the sticky viscera that splattered onto the thirsty grass. All the while, Simone tucked young Oumou into her chest, doing her best to hide her baby from the horror just outside.

Oumou's fists clenched and she felt the rage boiling up inside of her, each hit a furious percussion burst to her heart. Leslie reached down to grip her shoulder firmly and shook his head. She looked up at him and cautiously grabbed on to his hand.

"I don't know how your powers would manifest in here, but I really would prefer not to die in my sleep." His words were flippant, but his discomfort was apparent. He radiated the same fury she felt in her core.

She was about to reply when there was an echoing crack from the center of the lynch mob.

"Oh shit," one of the Klansmen said. He leaned over the still form of Oumou's father.

"Is he dead?" another one asked.

A silent pause weighed heavy in the night air as one of the men knelt down to check. "Yes."

"Oh shit, oh shit, oh shit," a fourth man said. "I thought we were just here to rough him up!" He began to back away from the rest of the members.

"Silence," the leader said, grabbing hold of him. "If he's dead, he's dead. Nothing lost."

"Daddy," the young Oumou shouted, and wrestled in her mom's grip, slipping out of her arms and into the dark clearing. The

Klansmen parted awkwardly as she approached the body of her father on the ground.

Leslie's chest tightened as he watched Oumou realize that Jeremiah wouldn't be getting up to respond to her cries. He felt Oumou's grip tighten around his own. She was more than angry now. He heard her try to hide a sniffle and felt her move to wipe away a tear. *How do you comfort a child watching her father die?* he thought. In a small gesture, he squeezed her hand as tight as he could.

The scene splayed out in front of them barreled on. Young Oumou's cries had stifled, all screamed out or muffled because her face was pressed into the cloth of her father's shirt. The whole world fell quiet. And then the silence broke. With laughter. At first just one of the men did it. A deep, booming laugh. It didn't take long for the rest to join in with him. Some nervously at first, but eventually the whole group of men was laughing at the young girl crying over her dead father. Her mother had caught up with her finally, wrapping her arms around her in a tight embrace. One of the men reached for her mother, and that's when Oumou's past self snapped.

The scream was unlike anything Leslie had ever heard. He looked down at his Oumou and saw that she was gone. He looked back up, and there she was. No longer was the girl he watched the Oumou of ten years past. She screamed like the damned. The whole forest seemed to shake with her rage. The ground erupted as if blasted apart from within, whole trees creaked and snapped under her invisible force. It sounded like cannon fire.

The Klansmen didn't have time to react before the force of her psychic assault hit them. Neither did her mother. A shockwave rippled through the air, sending everyone around Oumou careening away from the epicenter. A particularly unfortunate Klansman was caught by a thick, low-hanging branch directly through his chest. Leslie winced as blood burst forth in a black fount from the wound. His white robes dripped a dark crimson. The rest of the men, smelling the copper tinge of death in the air, tried to flee into the forest. *Big mistake,* Leslie thought. The agonizing groan of a toppling tree quieted the screams of several men with an earthy *thunk.* Several more were swallowed by dark chasms, open and echoing with the sounds of their screams. And then, as if passed into the eye of a hurricane, the forest fell silent. Oumou kneeled, still clutching her father in the center of a ring of earth stripped bare of all grass. In the distance, trees still fell, screaming in low, aching moans. The house hadn't stood a chance. All that was still recognizable was the stone chimney, no longer atop the house but embedded a good two feet deep into the earth nearby.

Finally, Oumou released her father and teetered to her feet. Looking around, Leslie realized what would happen next. He couldn't reach Oumou in time. All he could do was look in the direction of the next catastrophe.

Oumou locked eyes with him and then followed his gaze. "Mom." The words came out as a breathy whisper.

Simone Beverly lay gasping against a tree shattered by the force of her impact. Her frightened eyes darted around, unable to focus on any one thing. Oumou approached her, and the woman began to inch away, grimacing at the pain. She pressed herself snug against the splintered tree trunk. She spat blood and saw that she had forced the gnarly root piercing her back to wedge itself even deeper inside her.

"Mom," Oumou said. "It's me."

"No," her mother shouted. "Stay back!"

"Mommy." Oumou's voice creaked like a broken door in an empty hallway.

Simone's eyes locked on her daughter. "Oumou?" A trickle of blood dripped from her mouth.

"It's me, Mom, it's me," Oumou repeated. "It's me."

The woman surveyed everything around her. "You did this..." The words were flat, without accusation, but also without warmth.

"I did," Oumou said, and to Leslie she seemed ten years younger once again, stumbling over words, tears and snot running down her face.

"My God..." Oumou didn't hear the words that came next. Her mother's voice trailed off into a clicking rattle before her breath ceased for good.

Oumou stood alone by the remains of her house, both parents dead on the ground. All she could do was stand and stare off into the darkness of the night. "I'm sorry," she said, though neither of them could hear her words.

* * *

Oumou bolted upright and barely missed slamming her head on the corner of the coffee table. She must have shifted in her sleep. Her sudden rousing startled Magnum. The dog squawked and huffed in exasperation. With a disapproving glare he sauntered off to the kitchen, his tail twitching as he walked.

"Sorry," Oumou said, her mouth a grim line cut across her downcast face.

Leslie woke up slowly a few minutes after her. He exhaled the word "fuck" as he rose and rubbed his eyes. "Head feels like a cinderblock stuffed with cotton." He cracked his neck right, then left, then cast a solemn look over at Oumou. "Damn it. I don't know what to say, kid."

"It was me," she whispered, climbing onto the couch and sitting like a statue. "I killed them." She looked down at her hands. "Just like the man in the robe." The image of his corpse flashed in her mind alongside the bodies of her parents.

"You didn't kill your dad," Leslie said. He immediately regretted saying.

Oumou flashed him a look that could have killed him if she wanted it to.

"Fuck," Leslie said. "What I'm trying to say is that none of that is your fault."

"How could it not be?" Oumou asked. "I tried to save my mother and she died. I tried to protect myself in the vineyard and killed someone. I tried to stop that *thing* and now everyone thinks I killed the reverend too." She clenched her fists. "Ever since I got away, all I've done is hurt people."

"And plenty of those people fully deserved it," Leslie said. Kids were not his strong point, and despite himself he was growing frustrated. For the second time in a matter of minutes, he regretted the words that came out of his mouth.

"Hurting people is bad!" Oumou shouted. The sofa she was sitting on cracked in half. "The doctors hurt me and now...now I hurt everybody."

"Sometimes you've got to hurt people," Leslie said. "Sometimes, you just *do* hurt people, whether you mean to or not. That doesn't make you bad."

"What do you know?" Oumou spat. "You *want* to hurt people."

Leslie's face darkened. "You live through what I've lived through, and yeah, you're gonna want to hurt some people. Probably end up wanting a lot of people dead too. You forgive those doctors who hurt you?"

Oumou glowered at him.

"Bet you haven't. Bet you won't," Leslie said. "Because it isn't that easy, is it?"

"No."

"And I bet secretly you hope that those people that killed your dad are dead too, don't you?"

"Yes."

"And you think that makes you bad?"

"Yes!" Oumou screamed. A framed photo fell off the wall to her right.

Leslie sucked his teeth. "Look," he said. His attempt to soften his tone hardly worked. "That stuff don't make you a bad person. Everyone feels like that at some point." He sat down on the other side of the fractured sofa. "You like killing people?"

"Of course not," Oumou said.

"Of course not," Leslie repeated. "You know why? Because you're not a bad person."

"I'm just like that demon," she said.

"I can assure you," Leslie said. "You are nothing like that thing."

"It kills people too."

"And I'm pretty damn sure it enjoys it...a lot," Leslie said.

"I can't control it," Oumou said. She balled her hands into fists so tight her body trembled. "Whenever I'm angry, or scared...it just...happens."

"It's self-defense," Leslie said. "Fight or flight. Just so happens that you default to fight, and you hit like a goddamn atom bomb. Not your fault."

"I need to control it," Oumou said. "Not get angry. Or scared."

Leslie looked over at her with a quizzical look. "Wise words for someone as young as you, but let this old man do you one better. There's a time and place for control. Maybe in the forest that night. But that anger," he said, "that fear. That's powerful. Shit, if no one ever got angry, nothing would ever change, and you don't have the first clue how horrible that would be."

"I can't," Oumou said. "I'm too dangerous. It was right...I'm a monster, just like it."

"When I look at you," Leslie said, "do you know what I see?"

"What?"

"I see a girl put through the worst of it. You're terrified," he said. "Of everything. Don't bother lying about it. I'm a reporter, I get paid to see through bullshit. You're scared because you hurt people, and you're scared because people hurt you."

Oumou refused to meet his eye.

"You're just trying to survive, and people...man, people keep fucking with you. Testing you. And that gets them hurt." He walked over to the broken picture frame shattered on the floor and picked it up. "That's what I thought," he mumbled. He walked back to Oumou and tapped her gently on the shoulder. She looked up and he handed her the picture frame. "Only you get to decide what you are, kid," he continued. "You think you're a monster, that's what you'll turn out to be. But if you think you're something better...well, maybe you have a chance."

"You don't even know me," Oumou said.

"Look at the damn picture," Leslie said in an exasperated tone. "Moments like this ain't my thing. I'm really trying here."

Oumou looked down at the picture behind the shattered glass. "These are—"

"The people in that picture look nice," he said. "Much nicer than me. And I don't think their daughter could do anything at all that would convince them she was a monster."

"But you said the cabin in the dream was just—"

"Yeah, and I was wrong, okay? I told you straight up when you asked me that I don't know how this thing works all that well. Most of the time it's a nightmare I barely remember. This time it worked out like this."

"They look so happy," Oumou said. A glimmer of recognition flashed in her eyes. "That's me," she said.

"Looks just like the girl from the dream, so I'd say so," Leslie said.

Oumou struggled to keep a single emotion on her face. She wavered between happiness, sadness, anger, and confusion as Leslie watched. "They told me my parents got rid of me...because of my powers," she said. "That they didn't love me."

"And you're going to believe the people who made you suffer for most of your life?" Leslie asked.

"I didn't know anything else."

"And now you do," Leslie said.

"And now I know they're dead," Oumou said. "Because of me."

Leslie bit back a curse. *So much for progress*, he thought.

She glared up at him. "Why did you tell me this?"

"You asked." Leslie hit his limit and shouted back. "I told you that you might not like what you saw, but no, you had to know. Had to see your parents."

Oumou screamed. The front of the cabin cracked, and what remained of the front porch groaned and split straight down the middle. Without the support beams it sagged lower than it had before. Leslie flew backwards. His back slammed against the wall. He tried to move, but he was pinned by an invisible force.

He shouted over top of her scream. "Isn't this your problem?" he said. "You lash out and people die! So what? Am I next?"

Oumou's scream died down immediately. The rage drained from her face to be replaced by a guilty look that bordered on tears. Leslie fell to the floor with a *thud* and inhaled a fresh fog of previously undisturbed dust. He coughed violently as he stood and rubbed his back.

"Thank you for putting me down so gently," he said bitterly. He looked over and saw that Oumou had retreated to a position beside the sofa, almost out of view. Her knees were pulled to her chest, and she held the photo in her hands. He couldn't see her face, but he could hear the soft sounds of her crying.

Leslie let out an exaggerated sigh. He looked down at Magnum, who had sidled up to him. "I'm really not built for this," he said.

The dog raised his head and gave Leslie's hand a warm, slobbery lick.

"That's still disgusting," Leslie said. He walked over to the half of the couch farther away from Oumou and plopped down. The angry creak from the splintered wood made him wince as he did, but the fragment held his weight.

"Anyone who faults you for doing what you need to do to survive in this fucked up world is a piece of shit," he said. "And you know what you do when you see a piece of shit in your path?"

Oumou didn't respond.

"You step right over it."

"Ha." Oumou's vocalization was half-hearted at best.

Leslie stared across the room to the kitchen where a half empty bottle of whiskey glistened in the midday light filtering in from the broken window. He considered going for it but decided that if he couldn't even keep his temper around the kid while sober, a drink was the last thing he needed. The responsibility made him grimace. A pregnant silence settled over the inside of the cabin. Neither of them spoke. Leslie realized that as much as he hated arguing with the girl, he hated the awkward silence more.

CHAPTER 15

THERE WAS A knock on the front door. Leslie silently thanked God for the break in the suffocating silence. He'd tried talking to Oumou again, but the girl remained silent. She clutched the picture of her parents in her hands, only looking up from time to time to glare at him.

"You get out of sight for a bit," he said to Oumou in a hushed voice. Even Magnum seemed to understand the potential danger, as he silently stalked to a better vantage point of the door and perched like a pointy-eared gargoyle.

Leslie once again cursed the lack of a peephole on the cabin door. He took a deep breath, put a hand on the gun at his hip, and swung the door wide open. His gun was pointed directly in the face of a waif-thin, bookish woman with brown hair and thin librarian glasses framing a frightened face. She smelled like paper and perfume.

"Hello," she squawked as she stared at the barrel of the gun.

"Hi," he said. "Can I...help you?"

"Um." She flicked her eyes between Leslie's face and the gun.

"Oh," Leslie said. He stowed the gun back in the waist of his pants. "Precautions, you know? We had a rough night."

"Yes, of course," Vicki said. "I'm actually here to see Oumou...if she's here."

Leslie raised an eyebrow at her.

"I'm a friend." She shuffled her feet back and forth. "Amanda sent me."

"I don't know any Amanda," Leslie said.

"I do," Oumou said as she stepped out from her hiding space behind the couch.

"How are you doing, Oumou?" Vicki asked. She stepped into the cabin and closed the door behind her. Leslie leaned up against the door and watched the interaction play out.

"What did Amanda want?" Oumou said. Her voice crackled with ice.

Vicki cast a questioning glance at Leslie.

"Don't expect you'll get much out of her. She's...struggling right now," he said.

"I can imagine," Vicki said.

"I doubt it," Leslie said.

Vicki turned back to Oumou. "Amanda wanted me to bring you something," she said. "To remind you of your friendship." She handed Oumou the copy of *Frog and Toad are Friends*. "It's her favorite book."

"I can't read it." Oumou stared down at the floor and felt her face grow hot. "I never learned how."

"That's okay," Vicki said. "The important thing is that the two main characters are best friends, just like you and Amanda."

Oumou's eyes widened as she stared at the faded green cover of the book. She cradled it gently like a parent would hold a child. She didn't say anything, but a small smile spread across her face as she flipped through the pages, seeing image after image of the two creatures partaking in fun adventures. She opened her mouth to say "Thank you" when—

"Surprise!" Amanda shouted. She stood in the doorway with her arms raised dramatically. "I missed you so much, Oumou," she said as she rushed into the house and wrapped her arms around her friend. She let go and turned to Vicki. "Thank you for bringing me here."

"Amanda?" Vicki said. "How did...but I thought...oh, you tricked me. You devious little girl!" She placed a hand on her hip and waggled a disapproving finger at the blonde girl. "You shouldn't be here. What will your father think?"

"I don't know," Amanda said. "Probably something grumpy like 'You disobeyed me, young lady.'" She frowned sternly and imitated a deep voice that sounded nothing like her father's before she began to giggle mischievously.

Oumou could barely begin to form words. "Amanda..." She choked out her friend's name as a lump formed in her throat. "You came to see me? But I thought you... After your dad..." She trailed off.

"I gave him a stern talking to for making you leave," Amanda said, with her hands on her hips. "And then I asked Ms. Vicki to lead me here."

"That's one way of putting it," Vicki mumbled.

"Why?" Oumou said.

"I wanted to see my friend. And I was worried you might be scared. I'd be scared if I was out here alone." For the first time she noticed Leslie and Magnum, the dog who, after the first intrusion, had given up his attempts at being a guard dog. The dog sniffed at her acknowledgement.

"Oh," Amanda said, brightening so much she threatened to blind Oumou at such a close distance. "Puppy!"

Oumou didn't say anything. She grabbed Amanda in as tight of a hug as she could muster. "Thank you." She kept repeating. When she finally did let go, she looked into her friend's eyes and said, "I'm scared."

Amanda pondered this for a minute, chewing at her lower lip with an audible hum. "When I'm scared, I pretend I'm a superhero. Like in the comics my dad reads."

"Superhero?" Oumou asked.

"They're good guys with special powers who always save the day!" The blonde girl placed her hands on her hips and puffed out her chest.

Vicki and Leslie watched the exchange with a solemn amusement.

"But you don't have to pretend, because you *are* a superhero!" Amanda's smile flashed as bright as ever. "I've seen it. You can make things float." She proceeded to spin around and make whooshing noises. "Like that!"

"Superheroes are good," Oumou said. Doubt caused her voice to tremble. "What if I'm not good?"

"You are," Amanda said with a frown. "I wouldn't be friends with a bad guy."

"Really?"

"Yep!" Amanda said. "So, since we're friends, you must be good."

"That's certainly logic," Leslie whispered to Vicki, who shushed him.

"I don't know what's going on, but it seems like she needs this," she replied.

Oumou took a deep breath. "Okay, I'm good," she said to herself. "I am good." She looked at Leslie, who quirked an eyebrow in response. "I decide who I am, right?"

"That's what I said."

"I don't know if I'm good," Oumou said. "But Amanda thinks I am. Can I believe her?"

"Believing in the you that someone else believes in might get you through a bit, but eventually you'll have to believe in yourself," Leslie said. "You can't rely on other people's opinions forever."

Oumou nodded. "Okay. I believe you, Amanda. I am good."

"Yeah," Amanda said. "Believe in me!"

Oumou nodded. "Then in that case, I'm not a monster. I'm a superhero." She posed with her hands on her hips much like Amanda had just a few minutes ago. "One of the good guys. Amanda believes it" — she took a deep breath — "so I believe it."

Leslie laughed out loud. "Right, of course you are," he said. "And like all heroes, you'll make mistakes, and people will misunderstand you." There was no sarcasm in his voice, and he had a genuine smile on his face. "But you just gotta keep on trying to do good."

Oumou felt a weight rise from her shoulders. She was in a good mood for the first time since her and Amanda had played together in the vineyard. If they all believed it, maybe it was true. She turned to Leslie. "I'm sorry," she said. "For earlier."

"Yeah, me too," he said with a slight chuckle. "You're a good kid and I'm a shitty adult."

The good mood in the room dissipated as Magnum, who had been lounging silently in a nearby corner, began to grow agitated. He bared his fangs, and his normal low grumble of a warning turned into a furious bout of angry, terrified barks. The tirade ended with a full-on howl that trailed off into a whimper.

"What is the matter with you?" Leslie asked. "I've never seen you act like this before."

The dog's eyes were locked onto the open cellar door. Footsteps scraped against the wooden stairs as something ascended. A bloody hand emerged and grabbed onto the lip of the opening. It dug ragged fingernails into the wood and scraped across the panels as it pulled itself up and into the kitchen.

"Oh no," Leslie said. "Not now."

The bloody and disfigured body of the reverend stood in the doorframe between the kitchen and the living area. His face was cast in shadows despite the bright noon sun gleaming through the window, but Oumou could see that he had no eyes. He took a step towards them, not as a shambling corpse, but as he would if he were about to give a sermon. He turned his head towards the open front door, and slammed it shut so forcefully that cracks spider-webbed their way out from its frame.

"My God," Vicki said. "Reverend, is that you?"

"Greetings," the King of Thorns said to them. A cruel smile spread across his face. Black tendrils flickered out from his shadow like thorny snake tongues testing the air. He stepped into the room and regarded each of them with icy contempt. The body spread his arms wide and spoke in a booming voice. "And behold, a pale horse, and upon him a rider, the one called Death," he said with a blood-stained grin, "and Hell followed close behind. Within him was the power to kill by all means in heaven and Earth. I have come to strike down the evil of this Earth." The creature let out a hollow laugh. "Do I sound like that egotistical human?"

"You're possessing a corpse now?" Leslie asked. "That seems a bit beneath you."

"It seemed appropriate for this, our final encounter," the King of Thorns said as he turned to Oumou. "Now, will you surrender to me willingly, or will I be required to kill every person in this person and then take you by force?"

Oumou stepped in front of Amanda and ushered the other girl behind her. "I won't. I'm a superhero," she said. "I'm going to save the day."

The King of Thorns laughed. Blood sprayed from the reverend's mouth as he did. "Don't you get it, child? Your will is shaken. You can't fend me off this time."

"Fend off this," Leslie said. He drew his gun as fast as he could and fired. The bullet struck the King of Thorns right between the reverend's eyes. His head jerked backwards, and coagulated blood erupted onto the floor behind him. He slowly adjusted his head and leveled his eyeless gaze on Leslie.

"That was my plan," Leslie said. "I can say some prayers in a bunch of languages, but other than that—"

Black tendrils raced across the space between him and the King of Thorns, wrapping tight around his throat and raising him from the ground. Leslie gasped and choked. He kicked at the air and clawed at the bonds around his neck. His hands passed right through them and he scratched his own neck raw in the process.

"Reverend, please. Stop this nonsense," Vicki pleaded. "You can fight this...King of Thorns, and we can get you the help you need."

The King of Thorns turned to face Vicki, his face contorted in a mask of grief and fear. He dropped Leslie to the floor and took a hesitant step towards the woman. "Vicki...Porter?" he asked, reaching out a trembling hand. "Is that you?"

"Yes," Vicki said, tears in her eyes. "Yes, it's me. I'm here."

"I can't...see," he said. The creature's hand searched for her, fingers grasping as he slowly made his way towards her.

"Take my hand," Vicki said. "I'm right here."

"Vicki, don't do it," Leslie said. "It's not him."

"What do you mean?" Vicki turned towards Leslie. "He needs our—"

"Move!" Leslie roared.

Vicki turned back to the King of Thorns and saw that the fear on his face had been replaced with a mocking sneer. "The reverend's not here," he said.

Shadowy tendrils erupted from his eye sockets. They impaled Vicki right through her eyes. Expanding outwards, they tore her head apart and showered the floor with chunks of skull and brain matter.

Amanda screamed as blood poured out from the space where the woman's head had once been. The black tendrils receded back into the King of Thorns' eyes, and he wiped the blood that came with them away from his two gaping eye sockets.

"Besides," the King of Thorns said as he watched the body fall to the floor. "The dead can't help anyone."

"Son of a bitch!" Leslie shouted.

"Monster," Oumou said.

"Definitely," Leslie said through gritted teeth. "See the difference?"

"Yeah."

The house darkened with each step the King of Thorns took forward. He kept a leisurely pace, seeming to savor the mounting fear of everyone present as he approached. Bones clicked and creaked in the reverend's body as he walked. The King of Thorns raised his arms as if greeting a crowd, and Leslie collapsed to his knees with a shout of agony. He clutched at his skull and drove the palms of his hands into his ears. Oumou could hear the sounds of joints popping and bones creaking under an invisible force.

"Do you feel that?" the King of Thorns bellowed. "Do you feel what happens, Leslie Johnson, when you defy a god?"

"Fuck. You." Leslie said through gritted teeth. Blood vessels in his eyes popped, and blood poured from his nose.

A sharp howl followed by the quick pounding of footsteps drew the King of Thorns' attention just in time for Magnum to clamp his jaws around the man's throat.

Leslie gasped and rose unsteadily to his feet. "Thanks, boy."

With one quick motion, the dog tore out a chunk of the possessed man's throat and tossed it to the side, along with a slop of congealed blood. He bared his teeth and bit down again, this time aiming for the face.

The King of Thorns roared, a gargled hiss that caused more blood to cascade to the floor. "Filthy mongrel." Thorny tendrils wrapped around Magnum and pulled him off the creature's body. The chunk of his face trapped between Magnum's face tore away as they did. With a violent wave of the reverend's arms, Magnum was thrown across the room. The dog slammed into the wall with a pained yelp and slid to the floor. He coughed up a small splatter of blood, tried to stand back up, wobbled, and collapsed back to the floor. His eyes stared defiantly up at the King of Thorns, and his teeth still gleamed like knives from beneath curled-up lips.

"Hey," Leslie called. "That's my fucking dog." The gunshot echoed loudly in the cabin, blowing the already damaged portion of the body's skull clean off and revealing a now wounded brain. When the King of Thorns took a step towards him, Leslie fired again. This time he aimed for the knee. The King of Thorns dropped to the floor. "Human body, human limitations," Leslie said.

The King of Thorns rose back to his full height with a laugh. "You surprised me with that, but no," he said, "I have no such limitations."

"Oumou," Leslie said, "if you're going to do something, now would be the time."

Oumou let out a deep breath and summoned up all of her strength. Everything not bolted down in the cabin floated into the air and hung there as they awaited her command.

"Leave us alone!" Oumou thrust her arms forward. The assembled objects all slammed into the King of Thorns at once. Broken wood from chairs and tables impaled the body while furniture pressed in on it with a continuous groan. Oumou struggled as she held the items in place. She wanted to crush him until there was nothing left. Objects cracked and splintered under the force of her assault as they collapsed inward towards the King of Thorns. It was too much, and Oumou knew she couldn't hold it for much longer.

With a sound like a thunderclap, all of Oumou's assembled weapons were launched upward and blew a hole in the roof of the cabin. The King of Thorns, more bleeding muscle than flesh now, stood before her, unfazed. Oumou lashed out again, trying with all her might to force him away from her. The tatters of his robes and bloody flaps of hanging skin billowed as though caught in a hurricane.

"That's it?" the King of Thorns asked, taking a single step forward against the invisible force.

Oumou pushed harder, grinding her teeth until they felt ready to crack. The house groaned under the stress. Floorboards cracked and every window in the cabin shattered outward. Dust and wood fragments sprinkled onto the floor as the ceiling collapsed down to the inside. Oumou let out a gasp and clutched at her head as a wooden chunk of ceiling cracked her in the head. Her skull throbbed and wave after wave of vertigo washed over her. She struggled to remain upright.

"It appears we've seen all you can do with your power." The King of Thorns cracked his neck, breaking several vertebrae in the process. He righted his head and looked down on her with obvious disgust. "Pathetic."

"Why doesn't it work?" Oumou said. Sweat rolled down into her eyes as she panted and tried to catch her breath.

"It's simple," the creature said. "Your kind was not meant to wield such power."

"I have this power," Oumou said.

"You have nothing," he said with a sneer. "You accomplish nothing without throwing a tantrum. You waste your potential, and I've come to claim it."

"Hey, motherfucker," Leslie said, "looks to me like you're running out of time." Leslie waved his hands with a smug grin on his face.

The King of Thorns looked down at his ragged body. The body's remaining flesh was beginning to blister and melt away from the skeleton, dripping to the ground like candle wax.

"Like kindling," Leslie said.

The creature's face twisted in rage and an inhuman scream ripped from his torn mouth. Clawed, skeletal hands tore at the skin remaining on his face and ripped it down to the bloody bone.

"I will take what is mine!" he screamed as he lunged towards Oumou. "Mine!"

Leslie fired off another round, shattering the King of Thorns' other knee and sending him crashing to the floor. He looked up at him with nothing but fury in his eyes. Leslie pulled the trigger again, and the gun clicked; empty.

"Enough of you," he said.

Leslie let out a small cry of surprise as the thorny vines constricted around him and lifted him into the air. They held him there in the air, constricting until the sound of bones cracking filled the cabin.

"No!" Oumou shouted. She tried to rip apart the vines with her powers, but it didn't work. With a shout, she redirected her power at the King of Thorns, who deflected it with ease.

"Goodbye, Leslie Johnson," the creature said. He hurled Leslie into the kitchen. The man's back cracked against the granite countertop that protruded from the wall. His mouth opened in a silent scream, but all that came out was a rush of air from his lung. He took in a sharp breath, coughed blood onto his chest, and slumped over like he was sitting against the wall. His head lolled forward and he fell over completely. The rise and fall of his chest was barely noticeable.

With a whimper, Magnum half limped, half dragged his way over to Leslie. The dog licked his face a few times before positioning himself between the man and the monster. A low rumble escaped his chest.

Amanda ran for the door and tried the knob. No matter how hard she pulled, the door wouldn't budge. The King of Thorns raised a hand. His tendrils strung her up by her arms and pulled her to his side.

"So this is your friend," he said.

Amanda began to scream again, louder than before. The King of Thorns cast a disapproving glare on her and lashed her across the face. The shock of the blow stunned Amanda to silence and left a cut across her cheek that drooled red down to her chin.

"Leave her alone," Oumou said.

"You know what I want," he said.

"I don't want anyone to die."

"Anyone else, you mean," he said with a cruel smile.

"Yes."

"Then give me what I want." He extended his skeletal hand towards her.

"No, Oumou." Amanda choked out her words through her tears. "Save the day."

Oumou looked up at Amanda with a weak smile. "I can't," she said. "I'm not strong enough."

"I'm glad you understand your position," the King of Thorns said.

He clasped her arm in cold, bony fingers and pulled her in close. The smell of wet, decaying meat filled her head. Her stomach lurched. Amanda dropped unceremoniously to the floor below. She scrambled immediately to reach for Oumou, but the King of Thorns kicked her away.

Oumou was steeped in the creature's shadow, a dark presence with horns and claws. The shadow pulled itself away from the reverend's body and let the corpse tumble to the ground, truly dead.

The King of Thorns towered over Oumou. The room grew darker as his shadow pulled her deeper and deeper into the void. She felt his presence in her mind. With a sudden lurch, Oumou's vision went black.

CHAPTER 16

HAROLD ALWAYS THOUGHT he was a stoic individual, maybe cracking the odd joke or getting worked up here or there, but the sound coming from the cabin as his car screeched to a halt in the dirt driveway, the sound of his daughter screaming her throat raw from terror, put a panic in him that threatened to make his heart rupture in his chest. He flung the door to his car open so hard it nearly came off its hinges and he jumped out. He sprinted up the steps of the cabin's porch and slammed his shoulder into the flimsy wooden door with every ounce of his weight.

It didn't budge. He felt a sharp pop in the shoulder he led with and staggered back a step.

His wife was there a moment later. "What are you doing?" she said, her voice a high-pitched panic. "Open the door!"

"I hit it as hard as I could. An old door like this should've gone down easy," he said, nursing his shoulder and sizing up the door. "But—"

"Move," Elizabeth said, pushing him out of the way. She reared back and slammed the heel of her shoe against the door, just above the doorknob. The kick rebounded and Elizabeth stumbled backwards. Harold caught her just before she toppled over completely. She immediately pulled free from him and began pulling on the door with all of her strength.

"Why can't we get in?" Elizabeth screamed. She began to pound on the door. "Amanda, honey, can you hear me? Come open the door. Please. Honey." She pounded over and over but got no response from inside. Her shouts turned to sobs. She pressed her forehead against the door, no longer able to muster the energy to bang on the door. Amanda's screams didn't stop.

"What are we going to do?"

"Why can't she hear us?" Harold asked. He pulled his wife away from the door, afraid she might hurt herself if he left her there. "What is going on in there?"

"Damn it," Elizabeth said. She wrestled against her husband's grip, but he pulled her into a tight bear hug. "Let me go. Let me go, Harold!" She squirmed and jerked around, but he held her tight. "Our daughter is in there." She turned to pound her fists into his chest. "Let me go."

"We can't get the door down, you're just hurting yourself," he said as calmly as he could. His eyes drifted to the shattered window at the other end of the porch.

"I'll hurt myself all damn day to save my daughter! Let. Me. Go!"

"I'm going to try a different approach," Harold said. "If I let you go, do you promise to sit still?"

"No!" she shouted.

"Elizabeth, trust me," he said.

Elizabeth let out a shuddering breath. "Okay," she said. "Okay." Her body shook with the force of her sobbing even as she tried to quiet herself. "What are you going to do?"

"Windows are broken," he said. "I'm going to climb through."

"I'm coming too."

"No, honey, I don't think it'll be safe in there. Stay here."

The crunch of footsteps on gravel interrupted her disagreement. Harold turned to see Sylvia stumbling up the path. Her eyes were unfocused and darted around in a panic. It looked like she was muttering something. Her normal, perfect-postured walk had devolved into more of a hesitant shamble. A kitchen knife glinted in her hands.

"Sylvia?" Harold said, confused by her appearance. He took a hesitant step towards the woman, hands out in front of him in a placating manner.

In the short time since they'd left her, Sylvia's appearance had deteriorated further. Her hair, once always the epitome of prim, now sat in a tangled rat's nest above her pale, haggard face. Dark circles underscored her manic eyes that locked onto Harold as she approached. She stopped about three feet in front of him.

"Sylvia, what are you doing here?" Harold kept his tone calm and even. He forced himself not to glance towards the cabin, despite his daughter's screams.

"He called me," Sylvia said. "The King has called me here. My King of Thorns."

"Sylvia," he said. "As your doctor, I suggest you take a deep breath and go home."

Harold lunged at the woman as she moved to raise the knife. He tackled her to the ground with a shout. A sharp pain burned in his stomach. Blood trickled to the ground. Harold looked down at the knife buried up to the hilt in his lower abdomen. He'd grabbed her arm to keep her from thrusting, but as they fell...

He looked at the woman as his blood poured out onto her yellow blouse.

Sylvia sneered at him as she twisted the blade and carved it across his belly, spilling his steaming guts all over her. She rolled right and pushed him away, pulling the knife out as she did. Blood stained her arms up to the elbows, a color which smeared on her clothes as she stood and dusted herself off. She rubbed her hands down her face and peaked through her fingers with a laugh, Harold's blood streaking down her like war paint.

Elizabeth stared at the blood-soaked woman standing over her husband with horror. "Harold...?"

Sylvia looked at the dying man on the ground, then back to Elizabeth. For a split second, Elizabeth thought she saw recognition in Sylvia's eyes, but then it was gone. The woman screamed and sprinted at her with the knife, poised to strike.

Elizabeth couldn't move. Fear bolted her to the spot. But then there was something else. Her heartbeat pounded in her ears. She began to hyperventilate, and time seemed to slow down as the woman approached. Sylvia thrust out to stab her, and Elizabeth dropped. The woman tripped over her. Sylvia toppled forward and smashed her head into the unyielding door with a wet crunch.

Elizabeth scurried back to her feet and away from the woman lying on the porch nursing a now re-broken nose. She staggered to her husband's side and dropped to her knees.

"Harold," she said.

"Liz." A fit of bloody coughs wracked his body. "Hi."

"Tell me you're gonna be okay."

He looked down at the blood and viscera hanging out of his body. "In my professional opinion," he said, "the prognosis is not good." His eyes fluttered. "She severed both of my intestines and punctured my stomach. The yellowish stuff is—"

"Shut up," Elizabeth said. "Don't tell me that."

"Sorry, just...trying to stay calm. Doesn't hurt so much if I don't think about it, you know?" He grimaced as he spoke.

She started to reach towards the open wound, but pulled her hand away at the last minute, realizing it wasn't a good idea. "It looks like it hurts."

"It does. A lot."

"What can I do?"

"Hold my hand."

"Okay."

"Say a prayer for me?"

"You don't believe in God," she said. Tears stung her eyes as they rolled down her cheeks.

"No, but you do." His breathing grew shallow and each word struggled to make its way from his lips. "Take comfort in it."

"I don't know if I can." She squeezed his hand until hers shook and her knuckles whitened as if they were as devoid of blood as her husband. "How can anything comfort this?"

He whispered something inaudible and his eyes lost all focus. Shallow breaths faded to silence.

"Harold?" She shook him.

No response.

Again.

Nothing.

She pulled his body close and cradled him in her arms. "I can't do this on my own," she said. "I can't."

Elizabeth heard Sylvia's footsteps a second too late. The knife plunged into her shoulder. She screamed and scrambled away. Her motion ripped the knife from Sylvia's hand. Elizabeth gingerly fingered the wound as Sylvia stalked towards her.

The report of a gun made Elizabeth jump. Red blossomed fresh from Sylvia's shoulder. The woman shrieked. Her lips curled back over her teeth as she rounded on her assailant. A black police officer had his revolver aimed at Sylvia. Smoke still drifted from the barrel.

"Don't make me fire again, lady," he said.

An empty calm washed over Elizabeth. The pain in her shoulder faded to a dull ache. She reached back and pulled the knife free. Her blood glistened on the steel blade. The pounding of her heart slowed to an even rhythm as she laid Harold gently on the ground and rose to her feet. She wiped away her tears and stained her face with her husband's still warm blood.

"Sylvia," she said. All sound drained from the world, and all she could focus on was the woman who killed her husband.

Sylvia wheeled around with a hiss. Elizabeth jammed the knife into Sylvia's shoulder and ripped it back out just as quick. She tackled the woman to the ground, knife raised above her head, poised to impale it into her chest. Someone called out to her.

Harold? Is that you?

"Ma'am!" The police officer was shouting at her, the gun aimed not at Sylvia, but at her. "Put the knife down."

"She killed my husband," Elizabeth said. Her voice cracked as she spoke. "Ripped him open."

"I can see that," he said, his voice slow and even. "But I can't let you kill her, you know that." He took a step towards the two women. "Put the knife down."

"He's dead," Elizabeth shouted.

"And I am so, so sorry for your loss," he said as he took another step forward. "But if you don't put that knife down, I will be forced to shoot you. And I don't want that any more than you do."

Elizabeth's hands trembled. She dropped the knife to the side and stood up. With hesitation she stumbled backwards and stared down at the woman lying in a puddle of blood on the ground. "I'm sorry," she said, "I didn't mean — I don't — oh my God."

"You're all right," the police officer said. "My name is Carver McKay. Can you come over here?"

"Yes," Elizabeth said. "Yes, of course." She cast one last glance down at Harold laying on his back in the mud. She started walking towards Carver.

"Get down!" Carver shouted.

Elizabeth wasn't three steps into her walk, but when she heard that, she dropped to the ground, flattening her belly against the dirt. Two gunshots rang out over her head. She heard a sharp gasp followed by a heavy thud. Sylvia had fallen to the ground behind her, two new blooms of red spreading out from beneath her clothing.

Carver jogged over to Elizabeth and offered her a hand. She took it and felt the man's firm grip pull her to her feet.

"You shot her?" Elizabeth said.

"She was going to stab you from behind," Carver said.

"Thank you, then," Elizabeth said. "I'm sorry, who are you?"

"Carver McKay," he said. "I'm from the next town over."

"Yes, but... Why are you here?"

"I was following up on a promise I made to the man that lived here," he said. "Guess I picked the right time. What is going on?"

Elizabeth wiped her eyes and took a deep breath. "I honestly don't know, but my daughter is trapped in there. She was screaming, but" — she realized that she didn't hear Amanda anymore — "oh God, I think something happened to her. She isn't screaming anymore."

"She's in there?" Carver asked.

Elizabeth nodded.

"Well, let's get your daughter, ma'am."

"Elizabeth. Elizabeth Chastaine"

"Let's get your daughter, Mrs. Chastaine."

Carver climbed the steps to the front door, fired three shots into the space around the doorknob, and reared back to kick it in.

"I don't think—"

His boot slammed into the door with a loud thud. The door didn't budge. "Well, I'll be damned," he said.

"My husband and I tried breaking it down," Elizabeth said. "He was going to go in through the window before...before..."

"In through the window it is," Carver said.

CHAPTER 17

THE WORLD AROUND Oumou faded into existence like an image on a Polaroid picture. Her ears rang and her head swam as she gazed out into an endless expanse of darkness. She looked down at her arms and saw that she no longer had form or substance. Her entire body appeared as little more than a flat, white silhouette cut out from the pitch-black fabric of existence. She was no longer in the cabin, nor was she anywhere that she had ever seen before.

"Hello?" she called.

Her voice echoed back at her many times before finally dissipating into the silence from which it was borne. She looked up. Pinpricks of white glistened in the inky black tapestry of the sky, too far away to reach. All around her was the same, a stretch of darkness that ran all the way to where the horizon might be.

"Oumou."

"Hello?" Oumou asked again.

"Oumou," the voice said again.

"Where are you?"

"Oumou." The voice faded like the echo.

Everywhere looked the same, so with a shrug, Oumou set off walking in a random direction. No matter how far or long she walked, Oumou did not grow tired. She walked for what seemed like hours. Maybe it was days, she couldn't tell. Eventually she noticed a red glow flickering on the horizon. Her pace quickened. She came upon a pit of fire.

From her vantage point above the pit, she could see that there were people in the fire. They flailed and clawed at the air. She could hear their screams filling the air. A person near her looked up.

"You!" the person shouted. He began to climb the face of the cliff. Oumou could see a heavy chain attached to his ankle that ran its way back into the fire. Oumou stepped away from the edge of the pit as the man crawled his way over the lip. He looked up and she immediately recognized the hatred in his eyes.

The reverend lurched towards her. Oumou took a step back, but it didn't matter. The reverend reached the end of his length of chain and was jerked to the ground as he ran out of slack. He rose back to his feet and stared daggers at her.

"It's your fault that I'm here," he shouted. "You cursed me!"

"I didn't," Oumou said.

"I don't belong here," he said. Bloody tears poured down his face. "You belong here," he said. He reached out towards her. "Oh God, save me."

Oumou stepped away from the man.

"Don't leave me," he said. "It hurts. It hurts."

"I can't," Oumou said. She backed away from the pit and turned to run back in the other direction.

The reverend screamed after her. "Fuck you," he said. "You'll join me here one day. This is where you belong and you know it, you monster."

Oumou ran as hard and as fast as she could. She ran until the flickering orange light was nowhere to be seen. When she couldn't make it out on the horizon anymore, she stopped and sat on the ground.

"Oumou," the voice called out to her again.

"Who are you?" Oumou asked. "What do you want?"

"Walk," it said.

"I don't want to," Oumou said. "I'm scared." She looked off towards where the pit of fire had been. Despite her distance, she could still hear the people's screams, and she had to wonder why she hadn't heard them on her approach. She closed her eyes and tried to will the voices away. Silence swallowed the screams.

"Oumou?"

The voice was different. Closer. She opened her eyes and saw a man with a burnt face. He stood before her, his labcoat draped haphazardly over his thin frame. "Is it really you?" he asked.

Oumou bolted to her feet and stumbled away from the man. "No," she said. "Get away!"

The man held up his hands in surrender. "Whoa, whoa," he said. "I'm not going to hurt you."

"You already did!" Oumou shouted. She lashed out at the man with her mind, but nothing happened. Her powers didn't work here. She took another shaky step backwards. "Stay away."

Lawrence lowered his hands. A pained look crossed his face. "You're right," he said. "We did." He rubbed a hand through his shaggy hair. "I'd apologize, but I'm sure it wouldn't matter. And I doubt you'd accept it."

"I won't."

"That's fair," he said. "Can I sit?"

Oumou eyed him suspiciously. She nodded.

Lawrence sat down on the black ground and crossed his legs. "For what it's worth," he said, "and whether you accept it or not, I am sorry. Being here...I've had some time to think and...no matter how much we may have deluded ourselves, we were not the good guys."

"Where are we?" Oumou ignored his apology.

"I'm not quite sure," he said. "When I got here, I looked like you. A silhouette, not quite complete. I've wandered for quite some time and seen" — he looked off to the horizon — "well, I've seen a lot." He looked back at her. "Eventually I looked like my normal self again. All I can figure is this is some sort of limbo before the afterlife."

"I'm...dead?" Oumou asked.

"No, not yet. I imagine you'll know when you're dead because you'll look like me. Completely here. For now," he said, "I think you're just trapped."

"The monster got me," she said.

"Yeah, me too," Lawrence said. "Right after you escaped. Guess in retrospect I kind of deserved it." He stood up. "Well, I'm sure this wasn't a good experience for you, but it was nice seeing you, and I'm sorry...about the creature and everything."

Oumou looked away.

"Anyway," he said, "I think it's time for me to go." He turned towards the horizon. "I suggest you walk in the opposite direction of me. You'll prefer what you find over there." Lawrence began to walk away.

"Wait," Oumou said. "Don't go that way. It leads to—"

"I know," Lawrence said. "I know exactly where it leads." With that he set off walking towards the pit of fire with nothing but a wave over his shoulder. Oumou watched until the man's figure seemed to melt into the darkness, and then he was gone. Oumou sat alone for a while. She waited for the voice she'd heard before, but it didn't call out to her. She rose slowly, took a last glance towards the pit of fire, and set off in the opposite direction. Again she walked for a long time through the nondescript domain. This time, on the horizon she saw a bright white light that grew so bright as she approached that she soon found it hard to look forward.

A great golden gate ascended into view as she continued. It gleamed distinctly against the stark blackness around it. As the light of the gate fell upon her, Oumou was bathed in warmth. Her skin tingled and she was filled with peace. The gate was solid, and she couldn't see what lay beyond it, but she recognized the figure leaning up against it.

"Took you long enough," Leslie said. "I've been calling you."

"That was you?" Oumou said.

"Yeah, this shit's weird, but it kind of works like a dream, so I tried calling out to you. Results were obviously not perfect," he said with a wry smile. "But you're here now."

"Where's 'here'?"

"Don't worry about that yet," Leslie said. "You can't let that monster have you."

"It already got me," Oumou said dejectedly.

"Not completely," he said. "Look at you, just a silhouette still. He hasn't digested you yet."

"Digested?"

"You're not completely under his control yet."

"But I don't know how."

"How do you wake up from a dream?" Leslie asked.

"I don't know."

"Just like last time."

"But my powers don't work here," Oumou said.

"Mine do," Leslie said. "Maybe you've just got to try a little harder." He winked at her.

Oumou looked down at her hands and saw that they were beginning to resume their normal appearance. Leslie noticed too.

"Better hurry," he said.

Oumou stared at the golden gate. "Are you going in there?"

Leslie rapped a knuckle on the gate. "Not quite yet," he said. "But I have a feeling it'll be opening up for me soon."

"We can wake up together," Oumou said.

Leslie sucked his teeth. "I said *like* a dream, kid. This ain't a dream. You aren't waking up, you're breaking free. And I...I'm going to hang out right here."

"But—"

"Nope. Now get going," he said. He shooed her away. "Go wreak some havoc."

"Are you sure?" Oumou asked.

"Damn sure," he said. "Now go."

Oumou took a deep breath and turned her back on the man and the gate. Immediately she felt colder. The first step was the hardest. It felt like the gate was calling to her, beckoning her. With her second step, the warmth vanished all together. The third step was the hardest she'd ever taken, and with it the peace that had filled her so completely vanished. She felt hollow inside, but she continued forward. Something inside her said that if she turned around, she would run back to the gate and never leave the warmth of its glow. So she kept walking.

The gate's magnetic pull vanished, and she found herself back where she started. At least she thought it was where she started. It all looked the same. She stopped and turned a complete revolution. She saw neither the flickering flames of the pit nor the incandescence of the golden gate. She was alone.

"My powers don't work here," she mumbled. Leslie's words echoed in her mind. *Try harder.* She tightened her jaw and closed her eyes. "Fine." Her arms rose to her sides. She concentrated on everything around her. It looked like nothing, but it had to be something. She pulled against it.

Nothing.

Harder, she thought.

The ground trembled ever so slightly beneath her feet.

There.

She ground her teeth together, scrunched her eyes, and tightened every muscle in her body. The ground shook harder. Oumou struggled to stay upright as the earthquake roared all around her. The inky blackness began to crack, and beams of white light shone in. Streaked with light, the darkness began to dissipate.

"What do you think you're doing?" The King of Thorns appeared from out of the shadows with a sound like thunder. His shadowy form was illuminated by the rays of light seeping through the cracks in the world. Smoke curled from his jagged mouth, rising up over large horns. He exhaled a cloud of smoke that smelled like mildew. The cloud shrouded Oumou and made her sputter and gasp for air.

"I'm getting out," Oumou said. "I want my body back."

"Fool," he said with a sharp-toothed grin. "There is no escape. You are mine now."

The cracks in the world began to reseal, pulled together by the tendrils that spread out from the King of Thorns' body. Oumou struggled against his pull. A sweat broke out on her forehead. Her eyes stung as the salty liquid dripped down her face.

"You've already lost to me once," the demon said. "Why bother a second time? You are weak."

He was right. She was barely holding him off and the effort was draining her quickly. The light was fading fast, threatening to trap her in the darkness. Just like the Box. Oumou's pulse quickened. She thought of the lab and the experiments. The pain. The loneliness. The fear.

I won't go back, she thought.

She thought of the Chastaines and their kindness. She heard Amanda's voice in her head. *You're a superhero.* And she thought of the reverend and the fury and hate that drove him to attack her.

She thought of Leslie and Magnum still back in the real world. They needed her. *Maybe you're not trying hard enough,* his voice said.

She thought of her parents lying dead on the ground, of the men who attacked her in the vineyard, and of Amanda's broken-hearted face when Oumou gave up the fight in the cabin. The wound where the reverend shot her pulsed angrily and she felt the weight of Jim Buckett's boot on her chest. Oumou felt her fear fade, replaced with an all-consuming rage that burned her from within. She opened her mouth and let out a roar that rivaled the sound of the shattering world around her. Her eyes snapped open and locked on the King of Thorns, holding him in her fiery glare.

"I am *not* weak," she screamed.

The cracks in the world tore open at the sound of her voice. Blinding light poured into the world. The King of Thorns' empty sockets widened, and for the first time, Oumou saw fear in his eyes. His black tendrils covered in thorns began to evaporate as the shadows disappeared. Oumou raised her hands and the demon was dragged screaming into the empty sky. She clenched her fist and the light took on form. Chains of blinding light wrapped around the demon and constricted tighter and tighter until they tore through the shadowy fabric of his being.

Light continued to pour into the world until Oumou could no longer keep her eyes open. She clamped them shut and felt a lurch in her stomach, like she was falling from a great height. Her feet settled on solid ground, and she opened her eyes. The cabin assembled itself around her. It felt like something was forcing its way up her throat. She doubled over and clutched at her stomach. She gagged and retched and coughed as she tried to expel the obstruction.

"Oumou, are you all right?" Amanda took a hesitant step towards her.

Oumou held up a hand and pushed the girl away as gently as she could. Amanda toppled backwards and landed on her bottom. "Stay back," Oumou managed to choke out.

With a single violent choking noise, inky black fluid forced its way out of Oumou's mouth. It spilled onto the floor and rushed away from her. Slowly it began to take on a loose semblance of form. Pustules bubbled and popped all over the surface as the fluid took on the form of the King of Thorns.

"What have you done to me?" he gurgled. A dripping hand reached out towards Oumou. The demon's form melted apart before forming back together.

"I'm stronger than you," Oumou said as she wiped the remains of the black fluid from the corners of her mouth. "And you can't have me. No one can." The floor to the cabin split open. It widened into a great black fissure. "Not ever again."

The King of Thorns was pulled into the empty black of the fissure. He tried to hang on to the lip of the crevasse with formless claws that slipped off the splintered wood as he fell. Oumou gazed down into the darkness and saw the world from which she had escaped. Pinpricks of light gleamed up at her from the formless sky below. She watched as the King of Thorns descended into the abyss, screaming as he fell. The ground rumbled and Oumou took a step back, careful to avoid falling into the crevasse herself. With an ear-splitting noise, the crack in the floor sealed itself shut. The floor looked exactly as it had before, not a scratch or a sign of the opening remained. Oumou wobbled and collapsed to her knees. Her breaths came in deep heaving gasps. She looked over to Amanda.

"It's over," she said. "It's gone now."

Amanda rushed to her friend's side and wrapped her arms around her neck. "Are you okay?" She pulled away, but didn't let go, and stared intently into Oumou's eyes.

"I don't know," Oumou said. "I think so. I feel...good." She let a weak smile make its way across her face and pulled Amanda into a tight hug. When she let go, her attention was drawn to the kitchen by a wet cough.

"Leslie," Oumou said. She struggled to her feet and stumbled into the kitchen. Magnum rose to his feet and limped towards her. The dog pressed his cold nose into her arm. Oumou gave him a soft pet before moving him gently out of the way. "I need to get by," she said softly.

Leslie was slumped against the remains of the countertop. As she approached, his eyes fluttered open and he fixed her with an intense look. Oumou sat down beside him and stared out at the rest of the cabin. Her eyes scanned across the debris, lingered for a minute on Vicki Porter's body, and then made their way over to Amanda, who sat across from her, petting Magnum and giggling as he licked her face. Oumou was glad the dog was okay.

"See you took my advice," he said, his voice barely more than a whisper. "Made your way back." He tried to sit up straight, grimaced and sunk back down.

"It was just a dream," Oumou said. "So I woke up."

Leslie coughed out a laugh. "Something like that," he said.

"Is he going to be okay?" Amanda asked. She looked up from petting Magnum and gave Oumou a worried look.

"I've never been better, blondie," Leslie said. His breaths came in slow, laborious wheezes. A coughing fit wracked his body, causing a trickle of blood to run from the corners of his mouth. He was looking ahead with hazy eyes that didn't focus on anything. His fake smile trembled, and he couldn't maintain it for long. He turned his head to Oumou. She looked up at him.

"You fuck up that eyeless son of a bitch?" he asked.

Oumou frowned. "Fuck up?"

Leslie let out a disappointed sigh. "Yeah, shit, sorry. You beat him?"

"He's gone," Oumou answered. "I sent him to...wherever I was."

"Good, good. Won't be seeing him again, I guess." He closed his eyes and leaned his head back against the counter. "And good riddance too."

"Yeah," Oumou said.

"Oumou," Leslie wheezed.

"Yes?"

"Good work, kid," he rasped. "I think you may have just saved the world."

"Like a superhero," Oumou said.

"You're damn right," he said.

"It was because of you," she said.

"You're too humble," he said. "Own your shit. Take credit." He raised his fist and held it out to her. His hand trembled unsteadily.

Oumou looked at the fist, confused.

"Bump it," he said, "with your fist."

"Okay." Oumou did.

"Atta girl." Leslie's hand dropped to his side. "Have I mentioned that this shit hurts?"

"No."

"This shit hurts," he said with a weak grin. He let out a full body laugh that quickly transformed into a gasping spasm of pain. "And that hurt more. Lovely."

"I'm sorry," she said.

"Don't be," he said. "I got myself into this shit. Flew myself all the way down from New York to this ass-backwards town. Should've known better."

"I'm glad you were here," she said. "You helped me."

"Don't get all sentimental on me, kid," he said. "It upsets my stomach."

"Okay," she said, with a hint of sadness.

Leslie reached out and put a hand on her head. "I'm glad I was here too," he said. "Now I think...I have a golden gate to get back to." He looked up at the ceiling. "Haven't felt right since I left it."

"It was warm," Oumou said.

"Very warm," Leslie said. His eyes fluttered for a second and then closed. He sighed, a phlegmy, rasping sound that came from his chest, and then he fell silent.

"Leslie?"

Oumou hadn't known the man long enough to cry over him immediately, but her fist hung in the air where, for a brief instant, they had connected. She stared at the man, hoping that he would start breathing again. That he would sit up and tease her for being upset about him. But she knew that wasn't going to happen. She kept her fist there until it began to tremble, and the tears came, hot and blinding. It wasn't an uncontrollable sob. The tears trickled down her face and dripped silently onto the floor.

"Thank you," she said. She sat silently beside the man until Amanda toddled over to her side. The blonde girl tapped her on the shoulder.

"Is he—"

"He's dead," Oumou said softly.

"Was he your friend?"

"Yeah," Oumou said. "I think he was."

"I'm sorry."

Oumou looked up at her friend and saw tears forming in her eyes. "Why are you crying?"

"I'm sad for you," the blonde girl said. She sat down on the floor next to Oumou and patted her lap. Magnum trotted over and laid down in front of the girls. He rested his head in Oumou's lap and yawned in an exaggerated fashion. She stroked the dog between his ears.

A noise from the front of the cabin drew their attention. Magnum's ears pricked up and he turned to the front of the building. He rose to his feet and let out a low grumble. Oumou felt her pulse quicken.

It's gone, she thought. *It has to be.* Every fiber of her being was exhausted. She wasn't sure that she could stand if she tried, let alone put up a fight. She heard the crunch of glass. A black man, with a softer but more tired-looking face than Leslie, stepped into view.

CHAPTER 18

CARVER COULDN'T BELIEVE his eyes as he crawled in through the broken window. The cabin was a wreck on the inside. He counted two obvious corpses, one a woman with her head gone, and the other a man who looked as though he'd been through just about every kind of torture imaginable. Two girls sat on the floor next to a third body that he recognized as Leslie Johnson. He dropped to the floor and saw the dog as well. It grumbled at him for a minute but seemed to recognize him. The guttural sound stopped, and the dog began to pant excitedly. The girl with skin as dark as his struggled to her feet and fixed him with a threatening glare.

Carver raised his hands above his head. "I don't mean no harm," he said. "Look, the dog knows who I am, right, boy?"

Magnum barked a reply.

Carver slowly lowered his hands and took a step into the kitchen. "I take it you're Amanda," he said, nodding at the blonde girl still sitting on the floor.

"Yes," Amanda said with a soft sniffle.

"I got someone who really wants to see you," he said. "Ms. Elizabeth, it's safe for you to come in."

A few seconds later, Elizabeth was in the kitchen scooping her daughter into her arms and sobbing uncontrollably. Carver crossed the room and took Leslie's wrist in his hand.

"He's dead," Oumou said.

"Yes, it seems he is," Carver said. He took off his hat and put it on the countertop. "A damn shame." He looked at Oumou, who watched him with a suspicious eye. "Care to tell me what all happened here?"

"You wouldn't believe me," Oumou said.

Carver gazed around the room, taking in the brutal scene. "You wouldn't believe that you're the second person in so many days to tell me that, and this time I'm more inclined to believe what that person tells me."

Oumou glanced at Leslie's body. "He called it a demon," she said. "I fought a demon."

"A demon, huh?" Carver scratched at his head. "It do all this?" He gestured at the remains of the cabin interior with an airy hand.

"Not all of it," Oumou said.

Carver raised an eyebrow.

"I broke the furniture," she said. "It killed...everyone."

"You broke the furniture and fought a demon and...won?" he asked.

"She did," Amanda said. She pulled away from her mother and hopped to Oumou's side. "She's a superhero."

Oumou gave her friend a soft smile.

"You should show him," Amanda said. "He seems nice."

"I don't know," Oumou said, looking between the man and Mrs. Chastaine.

"Show him what?" Mrs. Chastaine asked, as she moved to be closer to her daughter and rested her hands on the girl's shoulders.

Oumou let out a deep sigh and raised her arms. The rubble and debris scattered around the interior of the cabin rose into the air at her command. With a circular motion, she set the objects swirling around. They circled around those gathered before clattering to the ground all at once. She lowered her arms with another exhalation.

"I can do that," she said.

Carver blinked in surprise. "That is something," he said.

"My God," Elizabeth gasped. "Why didn't you tell us about this before?"

"I didn't want to scare you," Oumou said. "And I didn't want you to send me back..."

"Back?" Elizabeth asked.

"To the lab. With the white coats and their experiments."

"Like science experiments?"

"They hurt me," Oumou said. "A lot."

"So you hid this?"

"To stay safe," Oumou said.

"She told me!" Amanda said. "Because I caught her doing it with apple slices at night."

"The juggling," Elizabeth said. "And why didn't you tell us, young lady?"

"Oumou made me promise to keep it a secret," the girl chirped. "Friends keep secrets for each other."

"Of course," Elizabeth sighed. "It could have been dangerous."

"Oumou isn't dangerous," Amanda said. "Not one bit."

"But all this..." Elizabeth surveyed the cabin with a grim countenance. "What you must have been through..."

"I was really scared," Amanda said. "But Oumou protected me. So it's okay now."

Oumou looked at Carver, still suspicious. "Are you going to take me back?"

"I wouldn't know where to take you if I wanted to," Carver said. "And I've had quite enough of good people being put through bad things of late." He wore a sad smile on his face, and reached out a hand to Oumou. "You can trust me," he said.

"Were you friends with Leslie?" Oumou asked.

Carver cast a remorseful look on the man's body. "I don't know if he would say as much, but I thought he was a good man. Troubled, but good."

"Then I trust you," Oumou said.

"What do we do now?" Elizabeth asked.

"Take my advice," Carver said. "Just go."

"Go?" Elizabeth asked. "Where?"

"Away from here," he said. "If what you say is true, then there are most likely people looking for you, and if they catch you, I can't imagine it would be pleasant." He holstered his gun. "You might not survive long enough to get away a second time."

"What about all this?" Elizabeth asked.

"I'll clean it up. Burn it. Leave as little trace as I can."

"Can you do that? Legally?"

"I'm tired of evidence being used to incriminate the wrong people and get them killed," he said. "So as far as I'm concerned, the fire was a freak accident."

"And Harold?" Elizabeth looked forlornly in the direction of her murdered husband.

"What happened to Daddy?" Amanda asked. She looked up at her mother with concern.

Tears ran down Elizabeth's face as she knelt next to her daughter. "He," she started. She swallowed hard. "Amanda, your father...he...he died. He's dead, sweetie."

The girl looked stunned. "But I just saw him this morning and he was fine."

"I know, sweetie, but some bad things happened and...he was protecting me, and..."

Amanda frowned as she tried to wrap her head around the information. She walked aimlessly around the kitchen and stared at the floor. "He's not coming back?"

"No. I'm so sorry, sweetie."

"Do you need a hug? I need a hug," Amanda said. She held out her arms towards her mother. Elizabeth spilled into her daughter's arms. She and Amanda cried in each other's arms for a few minutes before they separated. Amanda walked over to Oumou and pulled her into a hug as well. Oumou didn't cry, but she held her friend tight until she pulled away.

Elizabeth wiped her eyes and stood back up. "What about Harold's body?" she asked Carver.

"Does he have a will?"

"No."

"Then I say we burn him and the woman with the rest of the cabin." Carver gave a grim smile. "They both tie back to you, so it's for the best."

"Right," Elizabeth nodded. "Of course." She took Amanda by the hand.

"What about me?" Oumou asked. Her voice was a trembling whisper.

Carver looked between the black girl and Elizabeth.

"You protected Amanda?" she asked. "From" — she squeezed her eyes shut and breathed deeply — "the demon?"

"She did," Amanda said.

"Yes," Oumou said. "She's my best friend."

Elizabeth nodded slowly. "Okay."

"I can just go," Oumou said.

"No, no, that's not what I'm saying, it's just...a lot to take in." Elizabeth held out a hand to Oumou. "Of course you can come with us."

"Where are we going to go, Mom?" Amanda asked.

"I don't know. Where would you like to live?"

Amanda gasped. "Florida! We could go to the amusement park every day."

Elizabeth laughed out loud at the girl's excitement. "That's an idea," she said. "And what about you, Oumou? Any suggestions?"

"Anywhere is fine," Oumou said. "As long as I can stay with Amanda." She glanced over at Magnum, waiting in the crumbling doorframe. "He needs a home too."

"I'll take him," Carver said. "Don't you worry. After all, I am the one who raised him."

"But I thought—"

"That he was Leslie's dog? Well, the two of them did seem to get tangled up in each other's paths, but no, he's a police dog. My dog. I didn't take him last time I was here because I wanted him to protect Leslie." He looked forlornly at the man's body. "Guess it wasn't meant to be."

"Magnum did his best," Oumou said. "He fought for all of us."

Carver cleared his throat. "For now, how about you ladies head on outside. My truck's not too far away and I have some gas containers in the bed." He beckoned to Magnum. "Come on, boy, you can wait there while we handle this."

Magnum barked and bounded over to the cop's side, immediately dropping to a sitting position and panting up at the man. Carver scratched him behind the ears and under the chin.

"And you're sure you're okay with doing this for us?" Elizabeth asked.

"I really need to do some good today," Carver said. "I'll handle it."

* * *

"You know," Carver said, as he doused Leslie's body in gasoline. "I came back to tell you what happened." He picked up another gas container and poured it out all over the floor, being careful not to get any on his shoes. "Though I get the feeling you already knew how it would end. Hell, I did too, if I'm being honest." He wiped the sweat from his forehead and sat down against the counter beside Leslie's body. "I fought for him, you know. Told them all that the evidence didn't add up, but they didn't care. They wanted to hang him at noon, like something out of a bad Western movie." He blinked away the first couple of tears that threatened to roll down his face. "I did it," he said. "I don't know if it was better or worse, wrong or right, but I couldn't bear to let them have their sick fun. I couldn't bear to let the last thing he saw be the hatred in their eyes."

He let out a hoarse, humorless laugh. "The entire time, I ended up wondering what you would have done. Boy, you made quite an impression on me. I figured you'd have mouthed off at the lot of them and probably ended up dangling from a noose right alongside him." He stared down at his hands. "Well, I couldn't do that either. Did you know that they applauded me? I earned some twisted version of respect by putting an innocent man to death." He looked wearily at his silent companion. "It made me sick. I had to get away. Headed here." He squeezed Leslie's shoulder and rose to his feet. "Needed someone who'd understand my pain. Good thing, too. Saved that lady, and learned that, as it turns out, you weren't lying to me that night."

Carver stepped over the arranged bodies and stood on the porch. He faced into the cabin looking at the death and devastation. "Can't blame me for not believing you though," he said as he lit a match. "It was one hell of a story."

Carver tossed the match and watched the wooden structure go up in flames. The roaring heat of the fire licked at his face. He tipped his hat. "Take care, brother."

He stepped back and stood behind Elizabeth and the two young girls as they watched more of the house succumb to the flames. A low whistle escaped his lips.

"You may have overdid it on the gasoline."

Carver shook his head. "Gotta make sure everything is burned to hell so there's no chance of them identifying anyone. Y'all decide where you're going to go?" he asked.

Elizabeth nodded. "Yeah, we were thinking—"

Carver held up a hand. "Don't tell me. Plausible deniability and all that." He paused a moment. "Oumou, right?"

"Yeah," Oumou replied.

"Can I talk to you for a minute?" He motioned away from the group.

Oumou hesitated and looked at Mrs. Chastaine.

"Don't worry," she said. "I'll watch."

"Okay," Oumou said.

He walked her over to a quiet spot away from the heat of the burning cabin and knelt down in front of her. "You realize you've got to keep that power of yours a secret, right?"

"So I don't get caught."

"Yes, that," Carver said. "But also" — he took in a deep breath — "people are already gonna treat you different 'cause of your skin, as I'm sure you know."

"Right." Oumou stared at the ground. "I'm black."

"And don't you be ashamed of that," Carver said. He placed a hand on Oumou's shoulder. "Not now, not ever. And if they come after you, whoever they may be, girl, you fight as hard as you can to protect yourself." He smiled at her. "All I'm saying...all I'm asking," he said. "Is that you stay safe out there in this world, okay?"

Oumou smiled back. "I'll protect myself," she said, "and my new family too."

"Atta girl," he said, and watched as she skipped back over to Mrs. Chastaine and Amanda.

"I'm not afraid," she said.

"Of what?" Amanda asked.

"I don't know. Anything, I guess."

ACKNOWLEDGMENTS

A writer wanders into the void, with just a pen and an idea, hoping to create something new and wonderful. But there, in the dark, hungry things hide, hoping to bite and chew. And writers in particular are a delicacy to these creatures of the void. It is a dangerous endeavor that we choose to undertake, and it's even more dangerous to attempt it alone. In the dark, it's likely you'll get eaten.

I consider myself lucky to have so many people to take my trembling hand and lead me away from those gnashing teeth and barking cries.

Scarlett R. Algee has been fantastic to work with, not only for her patience in dealing with a new writer's thousands of questions, constant check-ins, and general flood of emails, but for her real and apparent excitement in working on *Touched by Shadows*. Her taking time to explain things and walk me through the publishing process as it progressed, while simultaneous sharing in my passion for the story, eased many fears and anxieties.

Thank you to S. A. Cosby, who, on our first meeting took a genuine interest in my story ideas and encouraged me to write what I want, and to do it with passion. I left that conference feeling my desire to write re-invigorated and truly believing that I could succeed.

Thank you to my friends Lauren and Luke, who took the burden of reading my roughest drafts, and offered in equal parts the constructive criticism I needed to improve and the praise necessary to my morale above rock bottom. You guys are great, and I hope you realize that you're now stuck in the place you've positioned yourselves as my go to beta readers.

To anyone else who had a hand in bringing this book to life, thank you. I appreciate your time, your effort, and your care. A book is made of many things and the words within are only one part. Your work should not go unacknowledged.

And finally, to Stephanie, who pushed and pushed and pushed, because she knew I could succeed. That I could reach this point. She believed in me, even when I didn't believe in myself. Without her, this novel may never have been submitted, so if you enjoy it, say a small thank you to her as well. I'll say the biggest 'Thank you,' right here.

ABOUT THE AUTHOR

Vaughn A. Jackson is a writer of speculative fiction, predominantly horror and giant monster fiction, and is a member of the Horror Writers Association. He is the author of both *Touched by Shadows* and *Up from the Deep*. His short story "The Thing at the Top of the Mountain" can be found in *Far From Home: An Anthology of Adventure Horror*. He wonders why whatever he writes always turns out at least somewhat scary, but doesn't believe in questioning things that work.

Vaughn lives near Baltimore with his girlfriend and two grumpy gremlins who disguise themselves as the cutest kittens in the world. His dog, Constantine, has demanded that she be included here as well. When he's not writing, he's probably doing something geeky because he is, at his core, a geek.

You can find Vaughn on Twitter via @blaximillion and on Instagram via @blaximillion_author.

www.ingramcontent.com/pod-product-compliance
Lightning Source LLC
Chambersburg PA
CBHW020657260626
47157CB00008B/3062